The Trail of the Goldseekers

The Trail of the Goldseekers

A Record of Travel in Prose and Verse

By

HAMLIN GARLAND

Author of

Rose of Dutcher's Coolly

Main Travelled Roads

Prairie Folks

Boy Life on the Prairie, etc.

New York

The Macmillan Company

London: Macmillan & Co., Ltd.

1899

Norwood Press
J. S. Cushing & Co. — Berwick & Smith
Norwood, Mass., U.S.A.

917.3

TABLE OF CONTENTS

128

Contents

POEMS

Contents

Contents

ANTICIPATION

I will wash my brain in the splendid breeze,
I will lay my cheek to the northern sun,
I will drink the breath of the mossy trees,
And the clouds shall meet me one by one.
I will fling the scholar's pen aside,
And grasp once more the bronco's rein,
And I will ride and ride and ride,
Till the rain is snow, and the seed is grain.

The way is long and cold and lone —
        But I go.
It leads where pines forever moan
   Their weight of snow,
        Yet I go.
There are voices in the wind that call,
There are hands that beckon to the plain;
I must journey where the trees grow tall,
And the lonely heron clamors in the rain.

Where the desert flames with furnace heat,
I have trod.
Where the horned toad's tiny feet
In a land
Of burning sand
Leave a mark,
I have ridden in the moon and in the dark.
Now I go to see the snows,
Where the mossy mountains rise
Wild and bleak — and the rose
And pink of morning fill the skies
With a color that is singing,
And the lights
Of polar nights
Utter cries
As they sweep from star to star,
Swinging, ringing,
Where the sunless middays are.

THE

TRAIL OF THE GOLDSEEKERS

CHAPTER I

COMING OF THE SHIPS

I

A LITTLE over a year ago a small steamer swung to at a Seattle wharf, and emptied a flood of eager passengers upon the dock. It was an obscure craft, making infrequent trips round the Aleutian Islands (which form the farthest western point of the United States) to the mouth of a practically unknown river called the Yukon, which empties into the ocean near the post of St. Michaels, on the northwestern coast of Alaska.

The passengers on this boat were not distinguished citizens, nor fair to look upon. They were roughly dressed, and some of them were pale and worn as if with long sickness or exhausting toil. Yet this ship and these passengers startled the whole English-speaking world. Swift as electricity could fly, the magical word GOLD went forth like a brazen eagle across the continent to turn the faces of millions of earth's toilers toward a region which, up to that time, had been unknown or of ill report. For this ship contained a million dollars in gold : these seedy passengers carried great bags of nuggets and bottles of shining dust which they had burned, at risk of their lives, out of the perpetually frozen ground, so far in the north that the winter had no sun and the summer midnight had no dusk.

The world was instantly filled with the stories of these men and of their tons of bullion. There was a moment of arrested attention — then the listeners smiled and nodded knowingly to each other, and went about their daily affairs.

But other ships similarly laden crept laggardly through the gates of Puget Sound, bringing other miners with bags and bottles, and then the world believed. Thereafter the journals of all Christendom had to do with the " Klondike " and " The Golden River." Men could not hear enough or read enough of the mysterious Northwest.

In less than ten days after the landing of the second ship, all trains westward-bound across America were heavily laden with fiery-hearted adventurers, who set their faces to the new Eldorado with exultant confidence, resolute to do and dare.

Miners from Colorado and cow-boys from Montana met and mingled with civil engineers and tailors from New York City, and adventurous merchants from Chicago set shoulder to shoemakers from Lynn. All kinds and conditions of prospectors swarmed upon the boats at Seattle, Vancouver, and other coast cities. Some entered upon new routes to the gold fields, which were now known to be far in the Yukon Valley, while others took the already well-known route by way of St. Michaels, and thence up the sinuous and sinister stream whose waters began on the eastern slope of the glacial peaks just inland from Juneau, and swept to the north and west for more than two thousand miles. It was understood that this way was long and hard and cold, yet thousands eagerly embarked on keels of all designs and of all conditions of unseaworthiness. By far the greater number assaulted the mountain passes of Skagway.

As the autumn came on, the certainty of the gold deposits deepened; but the tales of savage cliffs, of snow-walled trails, of swift and icy rivers, grew more numerous, more definite, and more appalling. Weak-hearted Jasons dropped out and returned to warn their friends of the dread powers to be encountered in the northern mountains.

As the uncertainties of the river route and the sufferings and toils of the Chilcoot and the White Pass became known, the adventurers cast about to find other ways of reaching the gold fields, which had come now to be called " The Klondike," because of the extreme richness of a small river of that name which entered the Yukon, well on toward the Arctic Circle.

From this attempt to avoid the perils of other routes, much talk arose of the Dalton Trail, the Taku Trail, the Stikeen Route, the Telegraph Route, and the Edmonton Overland Trail. Every town within two thousand miles of the Klondike River advertised itself as " the point of departure for the gold fields," and set forth the special advantages of its entrance way, crying out meanwhile against the cruel mendacity of those who dared to suggest other and "more dangerous and costly" ways.

The winter was spent in urging these claims, and thousands of men planned to try some one or the other of these "side-doors." The movement overland seemed about to surpass the wonderful transcontinental march of miners in '49 and '50, and those who loved the trail for its own sake and were eager to explore an unknown country hesitated only between the two trails which were entirely overland. One of these led from Edmonton to the head-waters of the Pelly, the other started from the Canadian Pacific Railway at Ashcroft and made its tortuous way northward between the great glacial coast range on the left and the lateral spurs of the Continental Divide on the east.

The promoters of each of these routes spoke of the beautiful valleys to be crossed, of the lovely streams filled with fish, of the game and fruit. Each was called "the poor man's route," because with a few ponies and a gun the prospector could traverse the entire distance during the summer, "arriving on the banks of the Yukon, not merely browned and hearty, but a veteran of the trail."

It was pointed out also that the Ashcroft Route led directly across several great gold districts and that the adventurer could combine business and pleasure on the trip by examining the Ominica country, the Kisgagash Mountains, the Peace River, and the upper waters of the Stikeen. These places were all spoken of as if they were close beside the trail and easy of access, and the prediction was freely made that a flood of men would sweep up this valley such as had never been known in the history of goldseeking.

As the winter wore on this prediction seemed about to be realized. In every town in the West, in every factory in the East, men were organizing parties of exploration. Grub stakers by the hundred were outfitted, a vast army was ready to march in the early spring, when a new interest suddenly appeared — a new army sprang into being.

Against the greed for gold arose the lust of battle. WAR came to change the current of popular interest. The newspapers called home their reporters in the North and sent them into the South, the Dakota cow-boys just ready to join the ranks of the goldseekers entered the army of the United States, finding in its Southern campaigns an outlet to their undying passion for adventure; while the factory hands who had organized themselves into a goldseeking company turned themselves into a squad of military volunteers. For the time the gold of the North was forgotten in the war of the South.

II

However, there were those not so profoundly interested in the war or whose arrangements had been completed before the actual outbreak of cannon-shot, and would not be turned aside. An immense army still pushed on to the north. This I joined on the 20th

day of April, leaving my home in Wisconsin, bound for
the overland trail and bearing a joyous heart. I believed that I was about to see and take part in a most
picturesque and impressive movement across the wilderness. I believed it to be the last great march of the
kind which could ever come in America, so rapidly were
the wild places being settled up. I wished, therefore, to
take part in this tramp of the goldseekers, to be one of
them, and record their deeds. I wished to return to the
wilderness also, to forget books and theories of art and
social problems, and come again face to face with the
great free spaces of woods and skies and streams. I
was not a goldseeker, but a nature hunter, and I was
eager to enter this, the wildest region yet remaining in
Northern America. I willingly and with joy took the
long way round, the hard way through.

CHAPTER II

OUTFITTING

WE went to sleep while the train was rushing past the lonely settler's shacks on the Minnesota Prairies. When we woke we found ourselves far out upon the great plains of Canada. The morning was cold and rainy, and there were long lines of snow in the swales of the limitless sod, which was silent, dun, and still, with a majesty of arrested motion like a polar ocean. It was like Dakota as I saw it in 1881. When it was a treeless desolate expanse, swept by owls and hawks, cut by feet of wild cattle, unmarred and unadorned of man. The clouds ragged, forbidding, and gloomy swept southward as if with a duty to perform. No green thing appeared, all was gray and sombre, and the horizon lines were hid in the cold white mist. Spring was just coming on.

Our car, which was a tourist sleeper, was filled with goldseekers, some of them bound for the Stikeen River, some for Skagway. While a few like myself had set out for Teslin Lake by way of " The Prairie Route." There were women going to join their husbands at Dawson City, and young girls on their way to Vancouver and Seattle, and whole families emigrating to Washington.

By the middle of the forenoon we were pretty well acquainted, and knowing that two long days were before us, we set ourselves to the task of passing the time. The women cooked their meals on the range in the forward part of the car, or attended to the toilets of the children, quite as regularly as in their own homes; while the men, having no duties to perform, played cards, or talked endlessly concerning their prospects in the Northwest, and when weary of this, joined in singing topical songs.

No one knew his neighbor's name, and, for the most part, no one cared. All were in mountaineer dress, with rifles, revolvers, and boxes of cartridges, and the sight of a flock of antelopes developed in each man a frenzy of desire to have a shot at them. It was a wild ride, and all day we climbed over low swells, passing little lakes covered with geese and brant, practically the only living things. Late in the afternoon we entered upon the Selkirks, where no life was.

These mountains I had long wished to see, and they were in no sense a disappointment. Desolate, death-haunted, they pushed their white domes into the blue sky in savage grandeur. The little snow-covered towns seemed to cower at their feet like timid animals lost in the immensity of the forest. All day we rode among these heights, and at night we went to sleep feeling the chill of their desolate presence.

We reached Ashcroft (which was the beginning of the long trail) at sunrise. The town lay low on the sand, a spatter of little frame buildings, mainly saloons and lodging houses, and resembled an ordinary cow-town in the Western States.

Rivers of dust were flowing in the streets as we debarked from the train. The land seemed dry as ashes, and the hills which rose near resembled those of Montana or Colorado. The little hotel swarmed with the rudest and crudest types of men; not dangerous men, only thoughtless and profane teamsters and cow-boys, who drank thirstily and ate like wolves. They spat on the floor while at the table, leaning on their elbows gracelessly. In the bar-room they drank and chewed tobacco, and talked in loud voices upon nothing at all.

Down on the flats along the railway a dozen camps of Klondikers were set exposed to the dust and burning sun. The sidewalks swarmed with outfitters. Everywhere about us the talk of teamsters and cattle men went on, concerning regions of which I had never heard. Men spoke of Hat Creek, the Chilcoten country, Soda Creek, Lake La Hache, and Lilloat. Chinamen in long boots, much too large for them, came and went sombrely, buying gold sacks and picks. They were mining quietly on the upper waters of the Fraser, and were popularly supposed to be getting rich.

The townspeople were possessed of thrift quite American in quality, and were making the most of the rush over the trail. "The grass is improving each day," they said to the goldseekers, who were disposed to feel that the townsmen were anything but disinterested, especially the hotel keepers. Among the outfitters of course the chief beneficiaries were the horse dealers, and every corral swarmed with mangy little cayuses, thin, hairy, and wild-eyed; while on the fences, in silent meditation or low-voiced conferences, the intending purchasers sat in rows like dyspeptic ravens. The wind storm continued, filling the houses with dust and making life intolerable in the camps below the town. But the crowds moved to and fro restlessly on the one wooden sidewalk, outfitting busily. The costumes were as various as the fancies of the men, but laced boots and cow-boy hats predominated.

As I talked with some of the more thoughtful and conscientious citizens, I found them taking a very serious view of our trip into the interior. "It is a mighty hard and long road," they said, "and a lot of those fellows who have never tried a trail of this kind will find it anything but a picnic excursion." They had known a few men who had been as far as Hazleton, and the tales of rain, flies, and mosquitoes which these adventurers brought back with them, they repeated in confidential whispers.

However, I had determined to go, and had prepared myself for every emergency. I had designed an insect-proof tent, and was provided with a rubber mattress, a down sleeping-bag, rain-proof clothing, and stout shoes. I purchased, as did many of the others, two bills of goods from the Hudson Bay Company, to be delivered at Hazleton on the Skeena, and at Glenora on the Stikeen. Even with this arrangement it was necessary to carry every crumb of food, in one case three hundred and sixty miles, and in the other case four hundred miles. However, the first two hundred and twenty miles would be in the nature of a practice march, for the trail ran through a country with occasional ranches where feed could be obtained. We planned to start with four horses, taking on others as we needed them. And for one week we scrutinized the ponies swarming around the corrals, in an attempt to find two packhorses that would not give out on the trail, or buck their packs off at the start.

"We do not intend to be bothered with a lot of mean broncos," I said, and would not permit myself to be deceived. Before many days had passed, we had acquired the reputation of men who thoroughly knew what they wanted. At least, it became known that we would not buy wild cayuses at an exorbitant price.

All the week long we saw men starting out with sore-backed or blind or weak or mean broncos, and heard many stories of their troubles and trials. The trail was said to be littered for fifty miles with all kinds of supplies.

One evening, as I stood on the porch of the hotel, I saw a man riding a spirited dapple-gray horse up the street. As I watched the splendid fling of his fore-feet, the proud carriage of his head, the splendid nostrils, the deep intelligent eyes, I said : "There is my horse! I wonder if he is for sale."

A bystander remarked, "He's coming to see you, and you can have the horse if you want it."

The rider drew rein, and I went out to meet him. After looking the horse all over, with a subtle show of not being in haste, I asked, "How much will you take for him?"

"Fifty dollars," he replied, and I knew by the tone of his voice that he would not take less.

I hemmed and hawed a decent interval, examining every limb meanwhile; finally I said, "Get off your horse."

With a certain sadness the man complied. I placed in his hand a fifty-dollar bill, and took the horse by the bridle. "What is his name?"

"I call him Prince."

"He shall be called Prince Ladrone," I said to Burton, as I led the horse away.

Each moment increased my joy and pride in my dapple-gray gelding. I could scarcely convince myself of my good fortune, and concluded there must be something the matter with the horse. I was afraid of some trick, some meanness, for almost all mountain horses are "streaky," but I could discover nothing. He was quick on his feet as a cat, listened to every word that was spoken to him, and obeyed as instantly and as cheerfully as a dog. He took up his feet at request, he stood over in the stall at a touch, and took the bit readily (a severe test). In every way he seemed to be exactly the horse I had been waiting for. I became quite satisfied of his value the following morning, when his former owner said to me, in a voice of sadness, "Now treat him well, won't you?"

"He shall have the best there is," I replied.

My partner, meanwhile, had rustled together three

packhorses, which were guaranteed to be kind and gentle, and so at last we were ready to make a trial. It was a beautiful day for a start, sunny, silent, warm, with great floating clouds filling the sky.

We had tried our tent, and it was pronounced a "jim-cracker-jack" by all who saw it, and exciting almost as much comment among the natives as my Anderson pack-saddles. Our "truck" was ready on the platform of the storehouse, and the dealer in horses had agreed to pack the animals in order to show that they were "as represented." The whole town turned out to see the fun. The first horse began bucking before the pack-saddle was fairly on, to the vast amusement of the by-standers.

"That will do for that beast," I remarked, and he was led away. "Bring up your other candidate."

The next horse seemed to be gentle enough, but when one of the men took off his bandanna and began binding it round the pony's head, I interrupted.

"That'll do," I said; "I know that trick. I don't want a horse whose eyes have to be blinded. Take him away."

This left us as we were before, with the exception of Ladrone. An Indian standing near said to Burton, "I have gentle horse, no buck, all same like dog."

"All right," said partner, with a sigh, "let's see him."

The "dam Siwash" proved to be more reliable than his white detractor. His horses turned out to be gentle and strong, and we made a bargain without noise. At

c

last it seemed we might be able to get away. "To-morrow morning," said I to Burton, "if nothing further intervenes, we hit the trail a resounding whack."

All around us similar preparations were going on. Half-breeds were breaking wild ponies, cow-boys were packing, roping, and instructing the tenderfoot, the stores swarmed with would-be miners fitting out, while other outfits already supplied were crawling up the distant hill like loosely articulated canvas-colored worms. Outfits from Spokane and other southern towns began to drop down into the valley, and every train from the East brought other prospectors to stand dazed and wondering before the squalid little camp. Each day, each hour, increased the general eagerness to get away.

From hot low sands aflame with heat,
   From crackling cedars dripping odorous gum,
I ride to set my burning feet
   On heights whence Uncompagre's waters hum,
From rock to rock, and run
      As white as wool.

My panting horse sniffs on the breeze
   The water smell, too faint for me to know;
But I can see afar the trees,
   Which tell of grasses where the asters blow,
And columbines and clover bending low
      Are honey-full.

I catch the gleam of snow-fields, bright
   As burnished shields of tempered steel,
And round each sovereign lonely height
   I watch the storm-clouds vault and reel,
Heavy with hail and trailing
      Veils of sleet.

" Hurrah, my faithful! soon you shall plunge
   Your burning nostril to the bit in snow;
Soon you shall rest where foam-white waters lunge
   From cliff to cliff, and you shall know
No more of hunger or the flame of sand
      Or windless desert's heat! "

CHAPTER III

ON THE STAGE ROAD

ON the third day of May, after a whole forenoon of packing and "fussing," we made our start and passed successfully over some fourteen miles of the road. It was warm and beautiful, and we felt greatly relieved to escape from the dry and dusty town with its conscience-less horse jockeys and its bibulous teamsters.

As we mounted the white-hot road which climbed sharply to the northeast, we could scarcely restrain a shout of exultation. It was perfect weather. We rode good horses, we had chosen our companions, and before us lay a thousand miles of trail, and the mysterious gold fields of the far-off Yukon. For two hundred and twenty miles the road ran nearly north toward the town of Quesnelle, which was the trading camp for the Caribou Mining Company. This highway was filled with heavy teams, and stage houses were frequent. We might have gone by the river trail, but as the grass was yet young, many of the outfits decided to keep to the stage road.

We made our first camp beside the dusty road near the stage barn, in which we housed our horses. A beautiful stream came down from the hills near us. A

21

little farther up the road a big and hairy Californian, with two half-breed assistants, was struggling with twenty-five wild cayuses. Two or three campfires sparkled near.

There was a vivid charm in the scene. The poplars were in tender leaf. The moon, round and brilliant, was rising just above the mountains to the east, as we made our bed and went to sleep with the singing of the stream in our ears.

While we were cooking our breakfast the next morning the big Californian sauntered by, looking at our little folding stove, our tent, our new-fangled pack-saddles, and our luxurious beds, and remarked: —

" I reckon you fellers are just out on a kind of little hunting trip."

We resented the tone of derision in his voice, and I replied: —

" We are bound for Teslin Lake. We shall be glad to see you any time during the coming fall."

He never caught up with us again.

We climbed steadily all the next day with the wind roaring over our heads in the pines. It grew much colder and the snow covered the near-by hills. The road was full of trampers on their way to the mines at Quesnelle and Stanley. I will not call them *tramps*, for every man who goes afoot in this land is entitled to a certain measure of respect. We camped at night just outside the little village called Clinton, which was not unlike a town in Vermont, and was established during the Caribou rush in '66. It lay in a lovely valley beside a swift, clear stream. The sward was deliciously green where we set our tent.

Thus far Burton had wrestled rather unsuccessfully with the crystallized eggs and evaporated potatoes which made up a part of our outfit. " I don't seem to get just the right twist on 'em," he said.

" You'll have plenty of chance to experiment," I remarked. However, the bacon was good and so was the graham bread which he turned out piping hot from the little oven of our folding stove.

Leaving Clinton we entered upon a lonely region, a waste of wooded ridges breaking illimitably upon the sky. The air sharpened as we rose, till it seemed like March instead of April, and our overcoats were grateful.

Somewhere near the middle of the forenoon, as we were jogging along, I saw a deer standing just at the edge of the road and looking across it, as if in fear of its blazing publicity. It seemed for a moment as if he were an optical illusion, so beautiful, so shapely, and so palpitant was he. I had no desire to shoot him, but, turning to Burton, called in a low voice, " See that deer."

He replied, " Where is your gun ? "

Now under my knee I carried a new rifle with a quantity of smokeless cartridges, steel-jacketed and soft-nosed, and yet I was disposed to argue the matter. " See here, Burton, it will be bloody business if we kill that deer. We couldn't eat all of it ; you wouldn't want to skin it ; I couldn't. You'd get your hands all bloody and the memory of that beautiful creature would not be pleasant. Therefore I stand for letting him go."

Burton looked thoughtful. "Well, we might sell it or give it away."

Meanwhile the deer saw us, but seemed not to be apprehensive. Perhaps it was a thought-reading deer, and knew that we meant it no harm. As Burton spoke, it turned, silent as a shadow, and running to the crest of the hill stood for a moment outlined like a figure of bronze against the sky, then disappeared into the forest. He was so much a part of nature that the horses gave no sign of having seen him at all.

At a point a few miles beyond Clinton most of the pack trains turned sharply to the left to the Fraser River, where the grass was reported to be much better. We determined to continue on the stage road, however, and thereafter met but few outfits. The road was by no means empty, however. We met, from time to time, great blue or red wagons drawn by four or six horses, moving with pleasant jangle of bells and the crack of great whips. The drivers looked down at us curiously and somewhat haughtily from their high seats, as if to say, "We know where we are going — do you know as much?"

The landscape grew ever wilder, and the foliage each day spring-like. We were on a high hilly plateau between Hat Creek and the valley of Lake La Hache. We passed lakes surrounded by ghostly dead trees, which looked as though the water had poisoned them. There were no ranches of any extent on these hills. The trail continued to be filled with tramping miners; several seemed to be without bedding or food. Some drove little pack animals laden with blankets, and all walked like fiends, pressing forward doggedly, hour after hour. Many of them were Italians, and one group which we overtook went along killing robins for food. They were a merry and dramatic lot, making the silent forests echo with their chatter.

I headed my train on Ladrone, who led the way with a fine stately tread, his deep brown eyes alight with intelligence, his sensitive ears attentive to every word. He had impressed me already by his learning and gentleness, but when one of my packhorses ran around him, entangling me in the lead rope, pulling me to the ground, the final test of his quality came. I expected to be kicked into shreds. But Ladrone stopped instantly, and looking down at me inquiringly, waited for me to scramble out from beneath his feet and drag the saddle up to its place.

With heart filled with gratitude, I patted him on the nose, and said, " Old boy, if you carry me through to Teslin Lake, I will take care of you for the rest of your days."

At about noon the next day we came down off the high plateau, with its cold and snow, and camped in a sunny sward near a splendid ranch where lambs were at play on the green grass. Blackbirds were calling, and we heard our first crane bugling high in the sky. From the loneliness and desolation of the high country, with its sparse road houses, we were now surrounded by sunny fields mellow with thirty seasons' ploughing.

The ride was very beautiful. Just the sort of thing

we had been hoping for. All day we skirted fine lakes with grassy shores. Cranes, ducks, and geese filled every pond, the voice of spring in their brazen throats.

Once a large flight of crane went sweeping by high in the sky, a royal, swift scythe reaping the clouds. I called to them in their own tongue, and they answered. I called again and again, and they began to waver and talk among themselves; and at last, having decided that this voice from below should be heeded, they broke rank and commenced sweeping round and round in great circles, seeking the lost one whose cry rose from afar. Baffled and angered, they rearranged themselves at last in long regular lines, and swept on into the north.

We camped on this, the sixth day, beside a fine stream which came from a lake, and here we encountered our first mosquitoes. Big, black fellows they were, with a lazy, droning sound quite different from any I had ever heard. However, they froze up early and did not bother us very much.

At the one hundred and fifty-nine mile house, which was a stage tavern, we began to hear other bogie stories of the trail. We were assured that horses were often poisoned by eating a certain plant, and that the mud and streams were terrible. Flies were a never ending torment. All these I regarded as the croakings of men who had never had courage to go over the trail, and who exaggerated the accounts they had heard from others.

We were jogging along now some fifteen or twenty miles a day, thoroughly enjoying the trip. The sky was radiant, the aspens were putting forth transparent yellow leaves. On the grassy slopes some splendid yellow flowers quite new to me waved in the warm but strong breeze. On the ninth day we reached Soda Creek, which is situated on the Fraser River, at a point where the muddy stream is deep sunk in the wooded hills.

The town was a single row of ramshackle buildings, not unlike a small Missouri River town. The citizens, so far as visible, formed a queer collection of old men addicted to rum. They all came out to admire Ladrone and to criticise my pack-saddle, and as they stood about spitting and giving wise instances, they reminded me of the Jurors in Mark Twain's "Puddin Head Wilson."

One old man tottered up to my side to inquire, "Cap, where you going?"

"To Teslin Lake," I replied.

"Good Lord, think of it," said he. "Do you ever expect to get there? It is a terrible trip, my son, a terrible trip."

At this point a large number of the outfits crossed to the opposite side of the river and took the trail which kept up the west bank of the river. We, however, kept the stage road which ran on the high ground of the eastern bank, forming a most beautiful drive. The river was in full view all the time, with endless vista of blue hills above and the shimmering water with radiant foliage below.

Aside from the stage road and some few ranches on the river bottom, we were now in the wilderness. On our right rolled a wide wild sea of hills and forests, breaking at last on the great gold range. To the west, a still wilder country reaching to the impassable east range. On this, our eighth day out, we had our second sight of big game. In the night I was awakened by Burton, calling in excited whisper, "There's a bear outside."

It was cold, I was sleepy, my bed was very comfortable, and I did not wish to be disturbed. I merely growled, " Let him alone."

But Burton, putting his head out of the door of the tent, grew still more interested. " There is a bear out there eating those mutton bones. Where's the gun?"

I was nearly sinking off to sleep once more and I muttered, " Don't bother me; the gun is in the corner of the tent." Burton began snapping the lever of the gun impatiently and whispering something about not being able to put the cartridge in. He was accustomed to the old-fashioned Winchester, but had not tried these.

" Put it right in the top," I wearily said, " put it right in the top."

" I have," he replied; " but I can't get it *in* or out!"

Meanwhile I had become sufficiently awake to take a mild interest in the matter. I rose and looked out. As I saw a long, black, lean creature muzzling at something on the ground, I began to get excited myself.

" I guess we better let him go, hadn't we?" said Burton.

" Well, yes, as the cartridge is stuck in the gun; and

so long as he lets us alone I think we had better let him alone, especially as his hide is worth nothing at this season of the year, and he is too thin to make steak."

The situation was getting comic, but probably it is well that the cartridge failed to go in. Burton stuck his head out of the tent, gave a sharp yell, and the huge creature vanished in the dark of the forest. The whole adventure came about naturally. The smell of our frying meat had gone far up over the hills to our right and off into the great wilderness, alluring this lean hungry beast out of his den. Doubtless if Burton had been able to fire a shot into his woolly hide, we should have had a rare " mix up " of bear, tent, men, mattresses, and blankets.

Mosquitoes increased, and, strange to say, they seemed to like the shade. They were all of the big, black, lazy variety. We came upon flights of humming-birds. I was rather tired of the saddle, and of the slow jog, jog, jog. But at last there came an hour which made the trouble worth while. When our camp was set, our fire lighted, our supper eaten, and we could stretch out and watch the sun go down over the hills beyond the river, then the day seemed well spent. At such an hour we grew reminiscent of old days, and out of our talk an occasional verse naturally rose.

MOMENTOUS HOUR

A coyote wailing in the yellow dawn,
A mountain land that stretches on and on,
And ceases not till in the skies
Vast peaks of rosy snow arise,
Like walls of plainsman's paradise.

I cannot tell why this is so;
I cannot say, I do not know
Why wind and wolf and yellow sky,
And grassy mesa, square and high,
Possess such power to satisfy.

But so it is.   Deep in the grass
I lie and hear the winds' feet pass;
And all forgot is maid and man,
And hope and set ambitious plan
Are lost as though they ne'er began.

A WISH

All day and many days I rode,
My horse's head set toward the sea;
And as I rode a longing came to me
That I might keep the sunset road,
Riding my horse right on and on,
O'ertake the day still lagging at the west,
And so reach boyhood from the dawn,
And be with all the days at rest.

For then the odor of the growing wheat,
The flare of sumach on the hills,
The touch of grasses to my feet
Would cure my brain of all its ills, —
Would fill my heart so full of joy
That no stern lines could fret my face.
There would I be forever boy,
Lit by the sky's unfailing grace.

CHAPTER IV

IN CAMP AT QUESNELLE

WE came into Quesnelle about three o'clock of the eleventh day out. From a high point which overlooked the two rivers, we could see great ridges rolling in waves of deep blue against the sky to the northwest. Over these our slender little trail ran. The wind was in the south, roaring up the river, and green grass was springing on the slopes.

Quesnelle we found to be a little town on a high, smooth slope above the Fraser. We overtook many prospectors like ourselves camped on the river bank waiting to cross.

Here also telegraph bulletins concerning the Spanish war, dated London, Hong Kong, and Madrid, hung on the walls of the post-office. They were very brief and left plenty of room for imagination and discussion.

Here I took a pony and a dog-cart and jogged away toward the long-famous Caribou Mining district next day, for the purpose of inspecting a mine belonging to some friends of mine. The ride was very desolate and lonely, a steady climb all the way, through fire-devastated forests, toward the great peaks. Snow lay in the road-side ditches. Butterflies were fluttering about, and in the high hills I saw many toads crawling over the snowbanks, a singular sight to me. They were silent, perhaps from cold.

Strange to say, this ride called up in my mind visions of the hot sands, and the sun-lit buttes and valleys of Arizona and Montana, and I wrote several verses as I jogged along in the pony-cart.

When I returned to camp two days later, I found Burton ready and eager to move. The town swarmed with goldseekers pausing here to rest and fill their parflêches. On the opposite side of the river others could be seen in camp, or already moving out over the trail, which left the river and climbed at once into the high ridges dark with pines in the west.

As I sat with my partner at night talking of the start the next day, I began to feel not a fear but a certain respect for that narrow little path which was not an arm's span in width, but which was nearly eight hundred miles in length. "From this point, Burton, it is business. Our practice march is finished."

The stories of flies and mosquitoes gave me more trouble than anything else, but a surveyor who had had much experience in this Northwestern country recommended the use of oil of pennyroyal, mixed with lard or vaseline. "It will keep the mosquitoes and most of the flies away," he said. "I know, for I have tried it. You can't wear a net, at least I never could. It is too warm, and then it is always in your way. You are in no danger from beasts, but you will curse the day you set out on this trail on account of the insects. It is the worst mosquito country in the world."

THE GIFT OF WATER

"Is water nigh?"
The plainsmen cry,
As they meet and pass in the desert grass.
With finger tip
Across the lip
I ask the sombre Navajo.
The brown man smiles and answers "Sho!"[1]
With fingers high, he signs the miles
To the desert spring,
And so we pass in the dry dead grass,
Brothers in bond of the water's ring.

MOUNTING

I mount and mount toward the sky,
The eagle's heart is mine,
I ride to put the clouds a-by
Where silver lakelets shine.
The roaring streams wax white with snow,
The eagle's nest draws near,
The blue sky widens, hid peaks glow,
The air is frosty clear.
And so from cliff to cliff I rise,
The eagle's heart is mine;
Above me ever broadning skies,
Below the rivers shine.

[1] Listen. Your attention.

THE EAGLE TRAIL

From rock-built nest,
The mother eagle, with a threatning tongue,
Utters a warning scream.   Her shrill voice rings
Wild as the snow-topped crags she sits among;
While hovering with her quivering wings
Her hungry brood, with eyes ablaze
She watches every shadow.   The water calls
Far, far below.   The sun's red rays
Ascend the icy, iron walls,
And leap beyond the mountains in the west,
And over the trail and the eagle's nest
The clear night falls.

CHAPTER V

THE PSYCHOLOGY OF THE BLUE RAT

Camp Twelve

NEXT morning as we took the boat — which was filled with horses wild and restless — I had a moment of exultation to think we had left the way of tin cans and whiskey bottles, and were now about to enter upon the actual trail. The horses gave us a great deal of trouble on the boat, but we managed to get across safely without damage to any part of our outfit.

Here began our acquaintance with the Blue Rat. It had become evident to me during our stay in Quesnelle that we needed one more horse to make sure of having provisions sufficient to carry us over the three hundred and sixty miles which lay between the Fraser and our next eating-place on the Skeena. Horses, however, were very scarce, and it was not until late in the day that we heard of a man who had a pony to sell. The name of this man was Dippy.

He was a German, and had a hare-lip and a most seductive gentleness of voice. I gladly make him historical. He sold me the Blue Rat, and gave me a chance to study a new type of horse.

Herr Dippy was not a Washington Irving sort of Dutchman; he conformed rather to the modern New York tradesman. He was small, candid, and smooth, very smooth, of speech. He said: "Yes, the pony is gentle. He can be rode or packed, but you better lead him for a day or two till he gets quiet."

I had not seen the pony, but my partner had crossed to the west side of the Fraser River, and had reported him to be a "nice little pony, round and fat and gentle." On that I had rested. Mr. Dippy joined us at the ferry and waited around to finish the trade. I presumed he intended to cross and deliver the pony, which was in a corral on the west side, but he lisped out a hurried excuse. "The ferry is not coming back for to-day and so —"

Well, I paid him the money on the strength of my side partner's report; besides, it was Hobson's choice.

Mr. Dippy took the twenty-five dollars eagerly and vanished into obscurity. We passed to the wild side of the Fraser and entered upon a long and intimate study of the Blue Rat. He shucked out of the log stable a smooth, round, lithe-bodied little cayuse of a blue-gray color. He looked like a child's toy, but seemed sturdy and of good condition. His foretop was "banged," and he had the air of a mischievous, resolute boy. His eyes were big and black, and he studied us with tranquil but inquiring gaze as we put the pack-saddle on him. He was very small.

"He's not large, but he's a gentle little chap," said I, to ease my partner of his dismay over the pony's surprising smallness.

"I believe he shrunk during the night," replied my partner. "He seemed two sizes bigger yesterday."

We packed him with one hundred pounds of our food and lashed it all on with rope, while the pony dozed peacefully. Once or twice I thought I saw his ears cross; one laid back, the other set forward, — bad signs, — but it was done so quickly I could not be sure of it.

We packed the other horses while the blue pony stood resting one hind leg, his eyes dreaming.

I flung the canvas cover over the bay packhorse. . . . Something took place. I heard a bang, a clatter, a rattling of hoofs. I peered around the bay and saw the blue pony performing some of the most finished, vigorous, and varied bucking it has ever been given me to witness. He all but threw somersaults. He stood on his upper lip. He humped up his back till he looked like a lean cat on a graveyard fence. He stood on his toe calks and spun like a weather-vane on a livery stable, and when the pack exploded and the saddle slipped under his belly, he kicked it to pieces by using both hind hoofs as featly as a man would stroke his beard.

After calming the other horses, I faced my partner solemnly.

"Oh, by the way, partner, where did you get that nice, quiet, little blue pony of yours?"

Partner smiled sheepishly. "The little divil. Buffalo Bill ought to have that pony."

"Well, now," said I, restraining my laughter, "the

thing to do is to put that pack on so that it will stay. That pony will try the same thing again, sure."

We packed him again with great care. His big, innocent black eyes shining under his bang were a little more alert, but they showed neither fear nor rage. We roped him in every conceivable way, and at last stood clear and dared him to do his prettiest.

He did it. All that had gone before was merely preparatory, a blood-warming, so to say; the real thing now took place. He stood up on his hind legs and shot into the air, alighting on his four feet as if to pierce the earth. He whirled like a howling dervish, grunting, snorting — unseeing, and almost unseen in a nimbus of dust, strap ends, and flying pine needles. His whirling undid him. We seized the rope, and just as the pack again slid under his feet we set shoulder to the rope and threw him. He came to earth with a thud, his legs whirling uselessly in the air. He resembled a beetle in molasses. We sat upon his head and discussed him.

" He is a wonder," said my partner.

We packed him again with infinite pains, and when he began bucking we threw him again and tried to kill him. We were getting irritated. We threw him hard, and drew his hind legs up to his head till he grunted. When he was permitted to rise, he looked meek and small and tired and we were both deeply remorseful. We rearranged the pack — it was some encouragement to know he had not bucked it entirely off — and by blindfolding him we got him started on the trail behind the train.

"I suppose that simple-hearted Dutchman is gloating over us from across the river,' said I to partner; "but no matter, we are victorious."

I was now quite absorbed in a study of the blue pony's psychology. He was a new type of mean pony. His eye did not roll nor his ears fall back. He seemed neither scared nor angry. He still looked like a roguish, determined boy. He was alert, watchful, but not vicious. He went off — precisely like one of those mechanical mice or turtles which sidewalk venders operate. Once started, he could not stop till he ran down. He seemed not to take our stern measures in bad part. He regarded it as a fair contract, apparently, and considered that we had won. True, he had lost both hair and skin by getting tangled in the rope, but he laid up nothing against us, and, as he followed meekly along behind, partner dared to say : —

"He's all right now. I presume he has been running out all winter and is a little wild. He's satisfied now. We'll have no more trouble with him."

Every time I looked back at the poor, humbled little chap, my heart tingled with pity and remorse. "We were too rough," I said. "We must be more gentle."

"Yes, he's nervous and scary; we must be careful not to give him a sudden start. I'll lead him for a while."

An hour later, as we were going down a steep and slippery hill, the Rat saw his chance. He passed into another spasm, opening and shutting like a self-acting jack-knife. He bounded into the midst of the peaceful horses, scattering them to right and to left in terror.

He turned and came up the hill to get another start. Partner took a turn on a stump, and all unmindful of it the Rat whirled and made a mighty spring. He reached the end of the rope and his hand-spring became a vaulting somersault. He lay, unable to rise, spatting the wind, breathing heavily. Such annoying energy I have never seen. We were now mad, muddy, and very resolute. We held him down till he lay quite still. Any well-considered, properly bred animal would have been ground to bone dust by such wondrous acrobatic movements. He was skinned in one or two places, the hair was scraped from his nose, his tongue bled, but all these were mere scratches. When we repacked him he walked off comparatively unhurt.

NOON ON THE PLAIN

The horned toad creeping along the sand,
The rattlesnake asleep beneath the sage,
Have now a subtle fatal charm.
In their sultry calm, their love of heat,
I read once more the burning page
Of nature under cloudless skies.
O pitiless and splendid land!
Mine eyelids close, my lips are dry
By force of thy hot floods of light.
Soundless as oil the wind flows by,
Mine aching brain cries out for night!

CHAPTER VI

THE BEGINNING OF THE LONG TRAIL

As we left the bank of the Fraser River we put all wheel tracks behind. The trail turned to the west and began to climb, following an old swath which had been cut into the black pines by an adventurous telegraph company in 1865. Immense sums of money were put into this venture by men who believed the ocean cable could not be laid. The work was stopped midway by the success of Field's wonderful plan, and all along the roadway the rusted and twisted wire lay in testimony of the seriousness of the original design.

The trail was a white man's road. It lacked grace and charm. It cut uselessly over hills and plunged senselessly into ravines. It was an irritation to all of us who knew the easy swing, the circumspection, and the labor-saving devices of an Indian trail. The telegraph line was laid by compass, not by the stars and the peaks; it evaded nothing; it saved distance, not labor.

My feeling of respect deepened into awe as we began to climb the great wooded divide which lies between the Fraser and the Blackwater. The wild forest settled around us, grim, stern, and forbidding. We were done with civilization.   Everything that was required for a home in the cold and in the heat was bound upon our five horses.   We must carry bed, board, roof, food, and medical stores, over three hundred and sixty miles of trail, through all that might intervene of flood and forest.

This feeling of awe was emphasized by the coming on of the storm in which we camped that night.   We were forced to keep going until late in order to obtain feed, and to hustle in order to get everything under cover before the rain began to fall.   We were only twelve miles on our way, but being wet and cold and hungry, we enjoyed the full sense of being in the wilderness.   However, the robins sang from the damp woods and the loons laughed from hidden lakes.

It rained all night, and in the morning we were forced to get out in a cold, wet dawn.   It was a grim start, dismal and portentous, bringing the realities of the trail very close to us.   While I rustled the horses out of the wet bush, partner stirred up a capital breakfast of bacon, evaporated potatoes, crystallized eggs, and graham bread.   He had discovered at last the exact amount of water to use in cooking these "vegetables," and they were very good.   The potatoes tasted not unlike mashed potatoes, aud together with the eggs made a very savory and wholesome dish.   With a cup of strong coffee and some hot graham gems we got off in very good spirits indeed.

It continued muddy, wet, and cold.   I walked most of the day, leading my horse, upon whom I had packed

a part of the outfit to relieve the other horses. There
was no fun in the day, only worry and trouble. My
feet were wet, my joints stiff, and my brain weary of
the monotonous black, pine forest.

There is a great deal of work on the trail,— cooking,
care of the horses, together with almost ceaseless packing and unpacking, and the bother of keeping the packhorses out of the mud. We were busy from five
o'clock in the morning until nine at night. There
were other outfits on the trail having a full ton of
supplies, and this great weight had to be handled four
times a day. In our case the toil was much less, but
it was only by snatching time from my partner that
I was able to work on my notes and keep my diary.
Had the land been less empty of game and richer in
color, I should not have minded the toil and care taking.
As it was, we were all looking forward to the beautiful
lake country which we were told lay just beyond the
Blackwater.

One tremendous fact soon impressed me. There
were no returning footsteps on this trail. All toes
pointed in one way, toward the golden North. No
man knew more than his neighbor the character of the
land which lay before us.

The life of each outfit was practically the same. At
about 4.30 in the morning the campers awoke. The
click-clack of axes began, and slender columns of pale
blue smoke stole softly into the air. Then followed
the noisy rustling of the horses by those set aside for
that duty. By the time the horses were " cussed into

camp," the coffee was hot, and the bacon and beans ready to be eaten. A race in packing took place to see who should pull out first. At about seven o'clock in the morning the outfits began to move. But here there was a difference of method. Most of them travelled for six or seven hours without unpacking, whereas our plan was to travel for four hours, rest from twelve to three, and pack up and travel four hours more. This difference in method resulted in our passing outfit after outfit who were unable to make the same distances by their one march.

We went to bed with the robins and found it no hardship to rise with the sparrows. As Burton got the fire going, I dressed and went out to see if all the horses were in the bunch, and edged them along toward the camp. I then packed up the goods, struck the tent and folded it, and had everything ready to sling on the horses by the time breakfast was ready.

With my rifle under my knee, my rain coat rolled behind my saddle, my camera dangling handily, my rope coiled and lashed, I called out, " Are we all set ? "

" Oh, I guess so," Burton invariably replied.

With a last look at the camping ground to see that nothing of value was left, we called in exactly the same way each time, " Hike, boys, hike, hike." (Hy-ak: Chinook for " hurry up.") It was a fine thing, and it never failed to touch me, to see them fall in, one by one. The " Ewe-neck " just behind Ladrone, after him " Old Bill," and behind him, groaning and taking on as if in great pain, " Major Grunt," while at the rear, with sharp outcry, came Burton riding the blue pony, who was quite content, as we soon learned, to carry a man weighing seventy pounds more than his pack. He considered himself a saddle horse, not a pack animal.

It was not an easy thing to keep a pack train like this running. As the horses became tired of the saddle, two of them were disposed to run off into the brush in an attempt to scrape their load from their backs. Others fell to feeding. Sometimes Bill would attempt to pass the bay in order to walk next Ladrone. Then they would *scrouge* against each other like a couple of country schoolboys, to see who should get ahead. It was necessary to watch the packs with worrysome care to see that nothing came loose, to keep the cinches tight, and to be sure that none of the horses were being galled by their burdens.

We travelled for the most part alone and generally in complete silence, for I was too far in advance to have any conversation with my partner.

The trail continued wet, muddy, and full of slippery inclines, but we camped on a beautiful spot on the edge of a marshy lake two or three miles in length. As we threw up our tent and started our fire, I heard two cranes bugling magnificently from across the marsh, and with my field-glass I could see them striding along in the edge of the water. The sun was getting well toward the west. All around stood the dark and mysterious forest, out of which strange noises broke.

In answer to the bugling of the cranes, loons were

E

wildly calling, a flock of geese, hidden somewhere under the level blaze of the orange-colored light of the setting sun, were holding clamorous convention. This is one of the compensating moments of the trail. To come out of a gloomy and forbidding wood into an open and grassy bank, to see the sun setting across the marsh behind the most splendid blue mountains, makes up for many weary hours of toil.

As I lay down to sleep I heard a coyote cry, and the loons answered, and out of the cold, clear night the splendid voices of the cranes rang triumphantly. The heavens were made as brass by their superb, defiant notes.

THE WHOOPING CRANE

At sunset from the shadowed sedge
    Of lonely lake, among the reeds,
He lifts his brazen-throated call,
    And the listening cat with teeth at edge
With famine hears and heeds.

" *Come one, come all, come all, come all !* "
Is the bird's challenge bravely blown
To every beast the woodlands own.

"*My legs are long, my wings are strong,*
    I wait the answer to my threat."
Echoing, fearless, triumphant, the cry
    Disperses through the world, and yet
Only the clamorous, cloudless sky
    And the wooded mountains make reply.

THE LOON

At some far time
This water sprite
A brother of the coyote must have been.
For when the sun is set,
Forth from the failing light
His harsh cries fret
The silence of the night,
And the hid wolf answers with a wailing keen.

CHAPTER VII

THE BLACKWATER DIVIDE

ABOUT noon the next day we suddenly descended to the Blackwater, a swift stream which had been newly bridged by those ahead of us. In this wild land streams were our only objective points; the mountains had no names, and the monotony of the forest produced a singular effect on our minds. Our journey at times seemed a sort of motionless progression. Once our tent was set and our baggage arranged about us, we lost all sense of having moved at all.

Immediately after leaving the Blackwater bridge we had a grateful touch of an Indian trail. The telegraph route kept to the valley flat, but an old trail turned to the right and climbed the north bank by an easy and graceful grade which it was a joy to follow. The top of the bench was wooded and grassy, and the smooth brown trail wound away sinuous as a serpent under the splendid pine trees. For more than three hours we strolled along this bank as distinguished as those who occupy boxes at the theatre. Below us the Blackwater looped away under a sunny sky, and far beyond, enormous and unnamed, deep blue mountains rose, notching the western sky. The scene was so exceedingly rich and amiable we could hardly believe it to be without farms and villages, yet only an Indian hut or two gave indication of human life.

After following this bank for a few miles, we turned to the right and began to climb the high divide which lies between the Blackwater and the Muddy, both of which are upper waters of the Fraser. Like all the high country through which we had passed this ridge was covered with a monotonous forest of small black pines, with very little bird or animal life of any kind. By contrast the valley of the Blackwater shone in our memory like a jewel.

After a hard drive we camped beside a small creek, together with several other outfits. One of them belonged to a doctor from the Chilcoten country. He was one of those Englishmen who are natural plainsmen. He was always calm, cheerful, and self-contained. He took all worry and danger as a matter of course, and did not attempt to carry the customs of a London hotel into the camp. When an Englishman has this temper, he makes one of the best campaigners in the world.

As I came to meet the other men on the trail, I found that some peculiar circumstance had led to their choice of route. The doctor had a ranch in the valley of the Fraser. One of " the Manchester boys " had a cousin near Soda Creek. " Siwash Charley " wished to prospect on the head-waters of the Skeena; and so in almost every case some special excuse was given. When the truth was known, the love of adventure had led all of us to take the telegraph route. Most of the miners argued that they could make their entrance by horse as cheaply, if not as quickly, as by boat. For the most part they were young, hardy, and temperate young men of the middle condition of American life.

One of the Manchester men had been a farmer in Connecticut, an attendant in an insane asylum in Massachusetts, and an engineer. He was fat when he started, and weighed two hundred and twenty pounds. By the time we had overtaken him his trousers had begun to flap around him. He was known as " Big Bill." His companion, Frank, was a sinewy little fellow with no extra flesh at all, — an alert, cheery, and vociferous boy, who made noise enough to scare all the game out of the valley. Neither of these men had ever saddled a horse before reaching the Chilcoten, but they developed at once into skilful packers and rugged trailers, though they still exposed themselves unnecessarily in order to show that they were not " tenderfeet."

" Siwash Charley " was a Montana miner who spoke Chinook fluently, and swore in splendid rhythms on occasion. He was small, alert, seasoned to the trail, and capable of any hardship. " The Man from Chihuahua " was so called because he had been prospecting in Mexico. He had the best packhorses on the trail, and cared for them like a mother. He was small, weazened, hardy as oak, inured to every hardship, and very wise in all things. He had led his fine little train of horses from Chihuahua to Seattle, thence to the Thompson River, joining us at Quesnelle. He was the typical trailer. He spoke in the Missouri fashion, though he was a born

Californian.   His partner was a quiet little man from Snohomish flats, in Washington.   These outfits were typical of scores of others, and it will be seen that they were for the most part Americans, the group of Germans from New York City and the English doctor being the exceptions.

There was little talk among us.   We were not merely going a journey, but going as rapidly as was prudent, and there was close attention to business.   There was something morbidly persistent in the action of these trains. They pushed on resolutely, grimly, like blind worms following some directing force from within.   This peculiarity of action became more noticeable day by day.   We were not on the trail, after all, to hunt, or fish, or skylark.   We had set our eyes on a distant place, and toward it our feet moved, even in sleep.

The Muddy River, which we reached late in the afternoon, was silent as oil and very deep, while the banks, muddy and abrupt, made it a hard stream to cross.

As we stood considering the problem, a couple of Indians appeared on the opposite bank with a small raft, and we struck a bargain with them to ferry our outfit. They set us across in short order, but our horses were forced to swim.   They were very much alarmed and shivered with excitement (this being the first stream that called for swimming), but they crossed in fine style, Ladrone leading, his neck curving, his nostrils wide-blown. We were forced to camp in the mud of the river bank, and the gray clouds flying overhead made the land exceedingly dismal.   The night closed in wet and cheerless.

The two Indians stopped to supper with us and ate heartily. I seized the opportunity to talk with them, and secured from them the tragic story of the death of the Blackwater Indians. "Siwash, he die hy-u (great many). Hy-u die, chilens, klootchmans (women), all die. White man no help. No send doctor. Siwash all die, white man no care belly much."

In this simple account of the wiping out of a village of harmless people by "the white man's disease" (small-pox), unaided by the white man's wonderful skill, there lies one of the great tragedies of savage life. Very few were left on the Blackwater or on the Muddy, though a considerable village had once made the valley cheerful with its primitive pursuits.

They were profoundly impressed by our tent and gun, and sat on their haunches clicking their tongues again and again in admiration, saying of the tent, "All the same lilly (little) house." I tried to tell them of the great world to the south, and asked them a great many questions to discover how much they knew of the people or the mountains. They knew nothing of the plains Indians, but one of them had heard of Vancouver and Seattle. They had not the dignity and thinking power of the plains people, but they seemed amiable and rather jovial.

We passed next day two adventurers tramping their way to Hazleton. Each man carried a roll of cheap quilts, a skillet, and a cup. We came upon them as they were taking off their shoes and stockings to wade through a swift little river, and I realized with a sudden pang of sympathetic pain, how distressing these streams must be to such as go afoot, whereas I, on my fine horse, had considered them entirely from an æsthetic point of view.

We had been on the road from Quesnelle a week, and had made nearly one hundred miles, jogging along some fifteen miles each day, camping, eating, sleeping, with nothing to excite us — indeed, the trail was quiet as a country lane. A dead horse here and there warned us to be careful how we pushed our own burden-bearers. We were deep in the forest, with the pale blue sky filled with clouds showing only in patches overhead. We passed successively from one swamp of black pine to another, over ridges covered with white pine, all precisely alike. As soon as our camp was set and fires lighted, we lost all sense of having travelled, so similar were the surroundings of each camp.

Partridges could be heard drumming in the lowlands. Mosquitoes were developing by the millions, and cooking had become almost impossible without protection. The " varments " came in relays. A small gray variety took hold of us while it was warm, and when it became too cold for them, the big, black, " sticky " fellows appeared mysteriously, and hung around in the air uttering deep, bass notes like lazy flies. The little gray fellows were singularly ferocious and insistent in their attentions.

At last, as we were winding down the trail beneath the pines, we came suddenly upon an Indian with a gun in the hollow of his arm. So still, so shadowy, so neutral in color was he, that at first sight he seemed a

part of the forest, like the shaded bole of a tree. He
turned out to be a "runner," so to speak, for the ferry-
men at Tchincut Crossing, and led us down to the outlet of the lake where a group of natives with their slim
canoes sat waiting to set us over. An hour's brisk
work and we rose to the fine grassy eastern slope overlooking the lake.

We rose on our stirrups with shouts of joy. We
had reached the land of our dreams! Here was the
trailers' heaven! Wooded promontories, around which
the wavelets sparkled, pushed out into the deep, clear
flood. Great mountains rose in the background, lonely,
untouched by man's all-desolating hand, while all about
us lay suave slopes clothed with most beautiful pea-
vine, just beginning to ripple in the wind, and beyond
lay level meadows lit by little ponds filled with wild-
fowl. There was just forest enough to lend mystery to
these meadows, and to shut from our eager gaze the
beauties of other and still more entrancing glades. The
most exacting hunter or trailer could not desire more
perfect conditions for camping. It was God's own
country after the gloomy monotony of the barren pine
forest, and needed only a passing deer or a band of elk
to be a poem as well as a picture.

All day we skirted this glorious lake, and at night we
camped on its shores. The horses were as happy as
their masters, feeding in plenty on sweet herbage for
the first time in long days.

Late in the day we passed the largest Indian village
we had yet seen. It was situated on Stony Creek,

which came from Tatchick Lake and emptied into Tchincut Lake. The shallows flickered with the passing of trout, and the natives were busy catching and drying them. As we rode amid the curing sheds, the children raised a loud clamor, and the women laughed and called from house to house, "Oh, see the white men!" We were a circus parade to them.

Their opportunities for earning money are scant, and they live upon a very monotonous diet of fish and possibly dried venison and berries. Except at favorable points like Stony Creek, where a small stream leads from one lake to another, there are no villages because there are no fish.

I shall not soon forget the shining vistas through which we rode that day, nor the meadows which possessed all the allurement and mystery which the word "savanna" has always had with me. It was like going back to the prairies of Indiana, Illinois, and Iowa, as they were sixty years ago, except in this case the elk and the deer were absent.

YET STILL WE RODE

We wallowed deep in mud and sand;
   We swam swift streams that roared in wrath;
They stood at guard in that lone land,
   Like dragons in the slender path.

Yet still we rode right on and on,
   And shook our clenched hands at the sky.
We dared the frost at early dawn,
   And the dread tempest sweeping by.

It was not all so dark.   Now and again
   The robin, singing loud and long,
Made wildness tame, and lit the rain
   With sudden sunshine with his song.

Wild roses filled the air with grace,
   The shooting-star swung like a bell
From bended stem, and all the place
   Was like to heaven after hell.

CHAPTER VIII

WE SWIM THE NECHACO

HERE was perfection of camping, but no allurement could turn the goldseekers aside. Some of them remained for a day, a few for two days, but not one forgot for a moment that he was on his way to the Klondike River sixteen hundred miles away. In my enthusiasm I proposed to camp for a week, but my partner, who was "out for gold instid o' daisies, 'guessed' we'd better be moving." He could not bear to see any one pass us, and that was the feeling of every man on the trail. Each seemed to fear that the gold might all be claimed before he arrived. With a sigh I turned my back on this glorious region and took up the forward march.

All the next day we skirted the shores of Tatchick Lake, coming late in the afternoon to the Nechaco River, a deep, rapid stream which rose far to our left in the snowy peaks of the coast range. All day the sky to the east had a brazen glow, as if a great fire were raging there, but toward night the wind changed and swept it away. The trail was dusty for the first time, and the flies venomous. Late in the afternoon we pitched camp, setting our tent securely, expecting rain. Before we went to sleep the drops began to drum on the tent

63

roof, a pleasant sound after the burning dust of the trail. The two trampers kept abreast of us nearly all day, but they began to show fatigue and hunger, and a look of almost sullen desperation had settled on their faces.

As we came down next day to where the swift Nechaco met the Endako rushing out of Fraser Lake, we found the most dangerous flood we had yet crossed. A couple of white men were calking a large ferry-boat, but as it was not yet seaworthy and as they had no cable, the horses must swim. I dreaded to see them enter this chill, gray stream, for not only was it wide and swift, but the two currents coming together made the landing confusing to the horses as well as to ourselves. Rain was at hand and we had no time to waste.

The horses knew that some hard swimming was expected of them and would gladly have turned back if they could. We surrounded them with furious outcry and at last Ladrone sprang in and struck for the nearest point opposite, with that intelligence which marks the bronco horse. The others followed readily. Two of the poorer ones labored heavily, but all touched shore in good order.

The rain began to fall sharply and we were forced to camp on the opposite bank as swiftly as possible, in order to get out of the storm. We worked hard and long to put everything under cover and were muddy and tired at the end of it. At last the tent was up, the outfit covered with waterproof canvas, the fire blazing and our bread baking. In pitching our camp we had plenty of assistance at the hands of several Indian boys from a near-by village, who hung about, eager to lend a hand, in the hope of getting a cup of coffee and a piece of bread in payment. The streaming rain seemed to have no more effect upon them than on a loon. The conditions were all strangely similar to those at the Muddy River.

Night closed in swiftly. Through the dark we could hear the low swish of the rising river, and Burton, with a sly twinkle in his eye, remarked, " For a semi-arid country, this is a pretty wet rain."

In planning the trip, I had written to him saying : " The trail runs for the most part though a semi-arid country, somewhat like eastern Washington."

It rained all the next day and we were forced to remain in camp, which was dismal business ; but we made the best of it, doing some mending of clothes and tackle during the long hours.

We were visited by all the Indians from Old Fort Fraser, which was only a mile away. They sat about our blazing fire laughing and chattering like a group of girls, discussing our characters minutely, and trying to get at our reasons for going on such a journey.

One of them who spoke a little English said, after looking over my traps : " You boss, you ty-ee, you belly rich man. Why you come ? "

This being interpreted meant, " You have a great many splendid things, you are rich. Now, why do you come away out here in this poor Siwash country ? "

I tried to convey to him that I wished to see the

F

mountains and to get acquainted with the people. He then asked, " More white men come ? "

Throwing my hands in the air and spreading my fingers many times, I exclaimed, " Hy-u white man, hy-u ! " Whereat they all clicked their tongues and looked at each other in astonishment. They could not understand why this sudden flood of white people should pour into their country. This I also explained in lame Chinook : " We go klap Pilchickamin (gold). White man hears say Hy-u Pilchickamin there (I pointed to the north). White man heap like Pilchickamin, so he comes."

All the afternoon and early evening little boys came and went on the swift river in their canoes, singing wild, hauntingly musical boating songs. They had no horses, but assembled in their canoes, racing and betting precisely as the Cheyenne lads run horses at sunset in the valley of the Lamedeer. All about the village the grass was rich and sweet, uncropped by any animal, for these poor fishermen do not aspire to the wonderful wealth of owning a horse. They had heard that cattle were coming over the trail and all inquired, " Spose when Moos-Moos come ? " They knew that milk and butter were good things, and some of them had hopes of owning a cow sometime.

They had tiny little gardens in sheltered places on the sunny slopes, wherein a few potatoes were planted; for the rest they hunt and fish and trap in winter and trade skins for meat and flour and coffee, and so live. How they endure the winters in such wretched houses, it is impossible to say. There was a lone white man living on the site of the old fort, as agent of the Hudson Bay Company. He kept a small stock of clothing and groceries and traded for " skins," as the Indians all call pelts. They count in skins. So many skins will buy a rifle, so many more will secure a sack of flour.

The storekeeper told me that the two trampers had arrived there a few days before without money and without food. " I gave 'em some flour and sent 'em on," he said. " The Siwashes will take care of them, but it ain't right. What the cussed idiots mean by setting out on such a journey I can't understand. Why, one tramp came in here early in the spring who couldn't speak English, and who left Quesnelle without even a blanket or an axe. Fact ! And yet the Lord seems to take care of these fools. You wouldn't believe it, but that fellow picked up an axe and a blanket the first day out. But he'd a died only for the Indians. They won't let even a white man starve to death. I helped him out with some flour and he went on. They all rush on. Seems like they was just crazy to get to Dawson — couldn't sleep without dreamin' of it."

I was almost as eager to get on as the tramps, but Burton went about his work regularly as a clock. I wrote, yawned, stirred the big campfire, gazed at the clouds, talked with the Indians, and so passed the day. I began to be disturbed, for I knew the power of a rain on the trail. It transforms it, makes it ferocious. The path that has charmed and wooed, becomes uncertain, treacherous, gloomy, and engulfing. Creeks become rivers, rivers impassable torrents, and marshes bottomless abysses. Pits of quicksand develop in most unexpected places. Driven from smooth lake margins, the trailers' ponies are forced to climb ledges of rock, and to rattle over long slides of shale. In places the threadlike way itself becomes an aqueduct for a rushing overflow of water.

At such times the man on the trail feels the grim power of Nature. She has no pity, no consideration. She sets mud, torrents, rocks, cold, mist, to check and chill him, to devour him. Over him he has no roof, under him no pavement. Never for an instant is he free from the pressure of the elements. Sullen streams lie athwart his road like dragons, and in a land like this, where snowy peaks rise on all sides, rain meant sudden and enormous floods of icy water.

It was still drizzling on the third day, but we packed and pushed on, though the hills were slippery and the creeks swollen. Water was everywhere, but the sun came out, lighting the woods into radiant greens and purples. Robins and sparrows sang ecstatically, and violets, dandelions, and various kinds of berries were in odorous bloom. A vine with a blue flower, new to me, attracted my attention, also a yellow blossom of the cow-slip variety. This latter had a form not unlike a wild sunflower.

Here for the first time I heard a bird singing a song quite new to me. He was a thrushlike little fellow, very shy and difficult to see as he sat poised on the tip of a black pine in the deep forest. His note was a clear cling-ling, like the ringing of a steel triangle. *Ching-aling*, *chingaling*, one called near at hand, and then farther off another answered, *ching*, *ching*, *chingaling-aling*, with immense vim, power, and vociferation.

Burton, who had spent many years in the mighty forests of Washington, said: "That little chap is familiar to me. Away in the pines where there is no other bird I used to hear his voice. No matter how dark it was, I could always tell when morning was coming by his note, and on cloudy days I could always tell when the sunset was coming by hearing him call."

To me his phrase was not unlike the metallic ringing cry of a sort of blackbird which I heard in the torrid plazas of Mexico. He was very difficult to distinguish, for the reason that he sat so high in the tree and was so wary. He was very shy of approach. He was a plump, trim little fellow of a plain brown color, not unlike a small robin.

There was another cheerful little bird, new to me also, which uttered an amusing phrase in two keys, something like *tee tay*, *tee tay*, *tee tay*, one note sustained high and long, followed by another given on a lower key. It was not unlike to the sound made by a boy with a tuning pipe. This, Burton said, was also a familiar sound in the depths of the great Washington firs. These two cheery birds kept us company in the gloomy, black-pine forest, when we sorely needed solace of some kind.

Fraser Lake was also very charming, romantic enough to be the scene of Cooper's best novels. The water was deliciously clear and cool, and from the farther shore great mountains rose in successive sweeps of dark green foothills. At this time we felt well satisfied with ourselves and the trip. With a gleam in his eyes Burton said, "This is the kind of thing our folks think we're doing all the time."

RELENTLESS NATURE

She laid her rivers to snare us,
She set her snows to chill,
Her clouds had the cunning of vultures,
Her plants were charged to kill.
The glooms of her forests benumbed us,
On the slime of her ledges we sprawled;
But we set our feet to the northward,
And crawled and crawled and crawled!
We defied her, and cursed her, and shouted:
" To hell with your rain and your snow.
Our minds we have set on a journey,
And despite of your anger we go! "

CHAPTER IX

THE FIRST CROSSING OF THE BULKLEY

WE were now following a chain of lakes to the source of the Endako, one of the chief northwest sources of the Fraser, and were surrounded by tumultuous ridges covered with a seamless robe of pine forests. For hundreds of miles on either hand lay an absolutely untracked wilderness. In a land like this the trail always follows a water-course, either ascending or descending it; so for some days we followed the edges of these lakes and the banks of the connecting streams, toiling over sharp hills and plunging into steep ravines, over a trail belly-deep in mud and water and through a wood empty of life.

These were hard days. We travelled for many hours through a burnt-out tract filled with twisted, blackened uprooted trees in the wake of fire and hurricane. From this tangled desolation I received the suggestion of some verses which I call " The Song of the North Wind." The wind and the fire worked together. If the wind precedes, he prepares the way for his brother fire, and in return the fire weakens the trees to the wind.

We had settled into a dull routine, and the worst feature of each day's work was the drag, drag of slow hours on the trail. We could not hurry, and we were forced to watch our horses with unremitting care in order to nurse them over the hard spots, or, rather, the soft spots, in the trail. We were climbing rapidly and expected soon to pass from the watershed of the Fraser into that of the Skeena.

We passed a horse cold in death, with his head flung up as if he had been fighting the wolves in his final death agony. It was a grim sight. Another beast stood abandoned beside the trail, gazing at us reproachfully, infinite pathos in his eyes. He seemed not to have the energy to turn his head, but stood as if propped upon his legs, his ribs showing with horrible plainness a tragic dejection in every muscle and limb.

The feed was fairly good, our horses were feeling well, and curiously enough the mosquitoes had quite left us. We overtook and passed a number of outfits camped beside a splendid rushing stream.

On Burns' Lake we came suddenly upon a settlement of quite sizable Indian houses with beautiful pasturage about. The village contained twenty-five or thirty families of carrier Indians, and was musical with the plaintive boat-songs of the young people. How long these native races have lived here no one can tell, but their mark on the land is almost imperceptible. They are not of those who mar the landscape.

On the first of June we topped the divide between the two mighty watersheds. Behind us lay the Fraser, before us the Skeena. The majestic coast range rose like a wall of snow far away to the northwest, while a near-by lake, filling the foreground, reflected the blue ridges of the middle distance — a magnificent spread of wild landscape. It made me wish to abandon the trail and push out into the unexplored.

From this point we began to descend toward the Bulkley, which is the most easterly fork of the Skeena. Soon after starting on our downward path we came to a fork in the trail. One trail, newly blazed, led to the right and seemed to be the one to take. We started upon it, but found it dangerously muddy, and so returned to the main trail which seemed to be more numerously travelled. Afterward we wished we had taken the other, for we got one of our horses into the quicksand and worked for more than three hours in the attempt to get him out. A horse is a strange animal. He is counted intelligent, and so he is if he happens to be a bronco or a mule. But in proportion as he is a thoroughbred, he seems to lose power to take care of himself — loses heart. Our Ewe-neck bay had a trace of racer in him, and being weakened by poor food, it was his bad luck to slip over the bank into a quicksand creek. Having found himself helpless he instantly gave up heart and lay out with a piteous expression of resignation in his big brown eyes. We tugged and lifted and rolled him around from one position to another, each more dangerous than the first, all to no result.

While I held him up from drowning, my partner "brushed in" around him so that he *could* not become submerged. We tried hitching the other horses to him in order to drag him out, but as they were saddle-horses, and had never set shoulder to a collar in their lives, they refused to pull even enough to take the proverbial setting hen off the nest.

Up to this time I had felt no need of company on the trail, and for the most part we had travelled alone. But I now developed a poignant desire to hear the tinkle of a bell on the back trail, for there is no " funny business " about losing a packhorse in the midst of a wild country. His value is not represented by the twenty-five dollars which you originally paid for him. Sometimes his life is worth all you can give for him.

After some three hours of toil (the horse getting weaker all the time), I looked around once more with despairing gaze, and caught sight of a bunch of horses across the valley flat. In this country there were no horses except such as the goldseeker owned, and this bunch of horses meant a camp of trailers. Leaping to my saddle, I galloped across the spongy marsh to hailing distance.

My cries for help brought two of the men running with spades to help us. The four of us together lifted the old horse out of the pit more dead than alive. We fell to and rubbed his legs to restore circulation. Later we blanketed him and turned him loose upon the grass. In a short time he was nearly as well as ever.

It was a sorrowful experience, for a fallen horse is a horse in ruins and makes a most woful appeal upon one's sympathies. I went to bed tired out, stiff and sore from pulling on the rope, my hands blistered, my nerves shaken.

As I was sinking off to sleep I heard a wolf howl, as though he mourned the loss of a feast.

We had been warned that the Bulkley River was a bad stream to cross, — in fact, the road-gang had cut a new trail in order to avoid it, — that is to say, they kept to the right around the sharp elbow which the river makes at this point, whereas the old trail cut directly across the elbow, making two crossings. At the point where the new trail led to the right we held a council of war to determine whether to keep to the old trail, and so save several days' travel, or to turn to the right and avoid the difficult crossing. The new trail was reported to be exceedingly miry, and that determined the matter — we concluded to make the short cut.

We descended to the Bulkley through clouds of mosquitoes and endless sloughs of mud. The river was out of its banks, and its quicksand flats were exceedingly dangerous to our pack animals, although the river itself at this point was a small and sluggish stream.

It took us exactly five hours of most exhausting toil to cross the river and its flat. We worked like beavers, we sweated like hired men, wading up to our knees in water, and covered with mud, brushing in a road over the quicksand for the horses to walk. The Ewe-necked bay was fairly crazy with fear of the mud, and it was necessary to lead him over every foot of the way. We went into camp for the first time too late to eat by daylight. It became necessary for us to use a candle inside the tent at about eleven o'clock.

The horses were exhausted, and crazy for feed. It

was a struggle to get them unpacked, so eager were they to forage. Ladrone, always faithful, touched my heart by his patience and gentleness, and his reliance upon me. I again heard a gray wolf howl as I was sinking off to sleep.

THE GAUNT GRAY WOLF

O a shadowy beast is the gaunt gray wolf!
And his feet fall soft on a carpet of spines;
Where the night shuts quick and the winds are cold
He haunts the deeps of the northern pines.

His eyes are eager, his teeth are keen,
As he slips at night through the bush like a snake,
Crouching and cringing, straight into the wind,
To leap with a grin on the fawn in the brake.

He falls like a cat on the mother grouse
Brooding her young in the wind-bent weeds,
Or listens to heed with a start of greed
The bittern booming from river reeds.

He's the symbol of hunger the whole earth through,
His spectre sits at the door or cave,
And the homeless hear with a thrill of fear
The sound of his wind-swept voice on the air.

ABANDONED ON THE TRAIL

A poor old horse with down-cast mien and sad wild eyes,
Stood by the lonely trail — and oh !
He was so piteous lean.
He seemed to look a mild surprise
At all mankind that we should treat him so.
How hardily he struggled up the trail
And through the streams
All men should know.
Yet now abandoned to the wolf, his waiting foe,
He stood in silence, as an old man dreams.
And as his master left him, this he seemed to say :
" You leave me helpless by the path ;
I do not curse you, but I pray
Defend me from the wolves' wild wrath ! "
And yet his master rode away !

CHAPTER X

DOWN THE BULKLEY VALLEY

As we rose to the top of the divide which lies between the two crossings of the Bulkley, a magnificent view of the coast range again lightened the horizon. In the foreground a lovely lake lay. On the shore of this lake stood a single Indian shack occupied by a half-dozen children and an old woman. They were all wretchedly clothed in graceless rags, and formed a bitter and depressing contrast to the magnificence of nature.

One of the lads could talk a little Chinook mixed with English.

"How far is it to the ford?" I asked of him.

"White man say, mebbe-so six, mebbe-so nine mile."

Knowing the Indian's vague idea of miles, I said:—

"How *long* before we reach the ford? Sit-kum sun?" which is to say noon.

He shook his head.

"Klip sun come. Me go-hyak make canoe. Me felly."

By which he meant: "You will arrive at the ford by sunset. I will hurry on and build a raft and ferry you over the stream."

With an axe and a sack of dried fish on his back and

a poor old shot-gun in his arm, he led the way down the trail at a slapping pace. He kept with us till dinner-time, however, in order to get some bread and coffee.

Like the *Jicarilla* Apaches, these people have discovered the virtues of the inner bark of the black pine. All along the trail were trees from which wayfarers had lunched, leaving a great strip of the white inner wood exposed.

" Man heap dry — this muck-a-muck heap good," said the young fellow, as he handed me a long strip to taste. It was cool and sweet to the tongue, and on a hot day would undoubtedly quench thirst. The boy took it from the tree by means of a chisel-shaped iron after the heavy outer bark has been hewed away by the axe.

All along the trail were tree trunks whereon some loitering young Siwash had delineated a human face by a few deft and powerful strokes of the axe, the sculptural planes of cheeks, brow, and chin being indicated broadly but with truth and decision. Often by some old camp a tree would bear on a planed surface the rude pictographs, so that those coming after could read the number, size, sex, and success at hunting of those who had gone before. There is something Japanese, it seems to me, in this natural taste for carving among all the Northwest people.

All about us was now riotous June. The season was incredibly warm and forward, considering the latitude. Strawberries were in bloom, birds were singing, wild roses appeared in miles and in millions, plum and cherry trees were white with blossoms — in fact, the splendor and radiance of Iowa in June. A beautiful lake occupied our left nearly all day.

As we arrived at the second crossing of the Bulkley about six o'clock, our young Indian met us with a sorrowful face.

"Stick go in chuck. No canoe. Walk stick."

A big cottonwood log had fallen across the stream and lay half-submerged and quivering in the rushing river. Over this log a half-dozen men were passing like ants, wet with sweat, "bucking" their outfits across. The poor Siwash was out of a job and exceedingly sorrowful.

"This is the kind of picnic we didn't expect," said one of the young men, as I rode up to see what progress they were making.

We took our turn at crossing the tree trunk, which was submerged nearly a foot deep with water running at mill-race speed, and resumed the trail, following running water most of the way over a very good path. Once again we had a few hours' positive enjoyment, with no sense of being in a sub-arctic country. We could hardly convince ourselves that we were in latitude 54. The only peculiarity which I never quite forgot was the extreme length of the day. At 10.30 at night it was still light enough to write. No sooner did it get dark on one side of the hut before it began to lighten on the other. The weather was gloriously cool, crisp, and invigorating, and whenever we had sound soil under our feet we were happy.

The country was getting each hour more superbly

mountainous. Great snowy peaks rose on all sides. The coast range, lofty, roseate, dim, and far, loomed ever in the west, but on our right a group of other giants assembled, white and stern. A part of the time we threaded our way through fire-devastated forests of fir, and then as suddenly burst out into tracts of wild roses with beautiful open spaces of waving pea-vine on which our horses fed ravenously.

We were forced to throw up our tent at every meal, so intolerable had the mosquitoes become. Here for the first time our horses were severely troubled by myriads of little black flies. They were small, but resembled our common house flies in shape, and were exceedingly venomous. They filled the horses' ears, and their sting produced minute swellings all over the necks and breasts of the poor animals. Had it not been for our pennyroyal and bacon grease, the bay horse would have been eaten raw.

We overtook the trampers again at Chock Lake. They were thin, their legs making sharp creases in their trouser legs — I could see that as I neared them. They were walking desperately, reeling from side to side with weakness. There was no more smiling on their faces. One man, the smaller, had the countenance of a wolf, pinched in round the nose. His bony jaw was thrust forward resolutely. The taller man was limping painfully because of a shoe which had gone to one side. Their packs were light, but their almost incessant change of position gave evidence of pain and great weariness.

I drew near to ask how they were getting along. The tall man, with a look of wistful sadness like that of a hungry dog, said, " Not very well."

" How are you off for grub ? "

" Nothing left but some beans and a mere handful of flour."

I invited them to a " square meal " a few miles farther on, and in order to help them forward I took one of their packs on my horse. I inferred that they would take turns at the remaining pack and so keep pace with us, for we were dropping steadily now — down, down through the most beautiful savannas, with fine spring brooks rushing from the mountain's side. Flowers increased; the days grew warmer; it began to feel like summer. The mountains grew ever mightier, looming cloudlike at sunset, bearing glaciers on their shoulders. We were almost completely happy — but alas, the mosquitoes ! Their hum silenced the songs of the birds; their feet made the mountains of no avail. The otherwise beautiful land became a restless hell for the unprotected man or beast. It was impossible to eat or sleep without some defence, and our pennyroyal salve was invaluable. It enabled us to travel with some degree of comfort, where others suffered martyrdom.

At noon Burton made up a heavy mess, in expectation of the trampers, who had fallen a little behind. The small man came into view first, for he had abandoned his fellow-traveller. This angered me, and I was minded to cast the little sneak out of camp, but his pinched and hungry face helped me to put up with him. I gave him a smart lecture and said, "I supposed you intended to help the other man, or I wouldn't have relieved you of a pound."

The other toiler turned up soon, limping, and staggering with weakness. When dinner was ready, they came to the call like a couple of starving dogs. The small man had no politeness left. He gorged himself like a wolf. He fairly snapped the food down his throat. The tall man, by great effort, contrived to display some knowledge of better manners. As they ate, I studied them. They were blotched by mosquito bites and tanned to a leather brown. Their thin hands were like claws, their doubled knees seemed about to pierce their trouser legs.

"Yes," said the taller man, "the mosquitoes nearly eat us up. We can only sleep in the middle of the day, or from about two o'clock in the morning till sunrise. We walk late in the evening — till nine or ten — and then sit in the smoke till it gets cold enough to drive away the mosquitoes. Then we try to sleep. But the trouble is, when it is cold enough to keep them off, it's too cold for us to sleep."

"What did you do during the late rains?" I inquired.

"Oh, we kept moving most of the time. At night we camped under a fir tree by the trail and dried off. The mosquitoes didn't bother us so much then. We were wet nearly all the time."

I tried to get at his point of view, his justification for such senseless action, but could only discover a sort of blind belief that something would help him pull through. He had gone to the Caribou mines to find work, and, failing, had pushed on toward Hazleton with a dim hope of working his way to Teslin Lake and to the Klondike. He started with forty pounds of provisions and three or four dollars in his pocket. He was now dead broke, and his provisions almost gone.

Meanwhile, the smaller man made no sign of hearing a word. He ate and ate, till my friend looked at me with a comical wink. We fed him staples — beans, graham bread, and coffee — and he slowly but surely reached the bottom of every dish. He did not fill up, he simply "wiped out" the cooked food. The tall man was not far behind him.

As he talked, I imagined the life they had led. At first the trail was good, and they were able to make twenty miles each day. The weather was dry and warm, and sleeping was not impossible. They camped close beside the trail when they grew tired — I had seen and recognized their camping-places all along. But the rains came on, and they were forced to walk all day through the wet shrubs with the water dripping from their ragged garments. They camped at night beneath the firs (for the ground is always dry under a fir), where a fire is easily built. There they hung over the flame, drying their clothing and their rapidly weakening shoes. The mosquitoes swarmed upon them bloodily in the shelter and warmth of the trees, for they had no netting or tent. Their meals were composed of tea, a few hastily stewed beans, and a poor quality of sticky camp bread.

Their sleep was broken and fitful. They were either too hot or too cold, and the mosquitoes gave way only when the frost made slumber difficult. In the morning they awoke to the necessity of putting on their wet shoes, and taking the muddy trail, to travel as long as they could stagger forward.

In addition to all this, they had no maps, and knew nothing of their whereabouts or how far it was to a human habitation. Their only comfort lay in the passing of outfits like mine. From such as I, they "rustled food" and clothing. The small man did not even thank us for the meal; he sat himself down for a smoke and communed with his stomach The tall man was plainly worsted. His voice had a plaintive droop. His shoe gnawed into his foot, and his pack was visibly heavier than that of his companion.

We were two weeks behind our schedule, and our own flour sack was not much bigger than a sachet-bag, but we gave them some rice and part of our beans and oatmeal, and they moved away.

We were approaching sea-level, following the Bulkley, which flows in a northwesterly direction and enters the great Skeena River at right angles, just below its three forks. Each hour the peaks seemed to assemble and uplift. The days were at their maximum, the sun set shortly after eight, but it was light until nearly eleven. At midday the sun was fairly hot, but the wind swept down from the mountains cool and refreshing. I shall not soon forget those radiant meadows, over which the far mountains blazed in almost intolerable splendor; it was too perfect to endure. Like the light of the sun lingering on the high peaks with most magical beauty, it passed away to be seen no more.

In the midst of these grandeurs we lost one of our horses. Whenever a horse breaks away from his fellows on the trail, it is pretty safe to infer he has "hit the back track." As I went out to round up the horses, "Major Grunt" was nowhere to be found. He had strayed from the bunch and we inferred had started back over the trail. We trailed him till we met one of the trampers, who assured us that no horse had passed him in the night, for he had been camped within six feet of the path.

Up to this time there had been no returning footsteps, and it was easy to follow the horse so long as he kept to the trail, but the tramper's report was positive — no horse had passed him. We turned back and began searching the thickets around the camp.

We toiled all day, not merely because the horse was exceedingly valuable to us, but also for the reason that he had a rope attached to his neck and I was afraid he might become entangled in the fallen timber and so starve to death.

The tall tramper, who had been definitely abandoned by his partner, was a sad spectacle. He was blotched by mosquito bites, thin and weak with hunger, and his clothes hung in tatters. He had just about reached the limit of his courage, and though we were uncertain of our horses, and our food was nearly exhausted, we gave him all the rice we had and some fruit and sent him on his way.

Night came, and still no signs of "Major Grunt." It began to look as though some one had ridden him away and we should be forced to go on without him. This losing of a horse is one of the accidents which make the trail so uncertain. We were exceedingly anxious to get on. There was an oppressive warmth in the air, and flies and mosquitoes were the worst we had ever seen. Altogether this was a dark day on our calendar.

After we had secured ourselves in our tents that night the sound of the savage insects without was like the roaring of a far-off hailstorm. The horses rolled in the dirt, snorted, wheeled madly, stamped, shook their heads, and flung themselves again and again on the ground, giving every evidence of the most terrible suffering. "If this is to continue," I said to my partner, "I shall quit, and either kill all my horses or ship them out of the country. I will not have them eaten alive in this way."

It was impossible to go outside to attend to them. Nothing could be done but sit in gloomy silence and listen to the drumming of their frantic feet on the turf as they battled against their invisible foes. At last, led by old Ladrone, they started off at a hobbling gallop up the trail.

"Well, we are in for it now," I remarked, as the footsteps died away. "They've hit the back trail, and we'll have another day's hard work to catch 'em and bring 'em back. However, there's no use worrying. The mosquitoes would eat us alive if we went out now. We might just as well go to sleep and wait till morning." Sleep was difficult under the circumstances, but we dozed off at last.

As we took their trail in the cool of the next morning, we found the horses had taken the back trail till they reached an open hillside, and had climbed to the very edge of the timber. There they were all in a bunch, with the exception of " Major Grunt," of whom we had no trace.

With a mind filled with distressing pictures of the lost horse entangled in his rope, and lying flat on his side hidden among the fallen tree trunks, there to struggle and starve, I reluctantly gave orders for a start, with intent to send an Indian back to search for him.

After two hours' smart travel we came suddenly upon the little Indian village of Morricetown, which is built beside a narrow cañon through which the Bulkley rushes with tremendous speed. Here high on the level grassy bank we camped, quite secure from mosquitoes, and surrounded by the curious natives, who showed us where to find wood and water, and brought us the most beautiful spring salmon, and potatoes so tender and fine that the skin could be rubbed from them with the thumb. They were exactly like new potatoes in the States. Out of this, it may be well understood, we had a most satisfying dinner. Summer was in full tide. Pieplant was two feet high, and strawberries were almost ripe.

Calling the men of the village around me, I explained in Pigeon-English and worse Chinook that I had lost a horse, and that I would give five dollars to the man who would bring him to me. They all listened attentively, filled with joy at a chance to earn so much money. At last the chief man of the village, a very good-looking fellow of twenty-five or thirty, said to me: "All light, me go, me fetch 'um. You stop here. Mebbe-so, klip-sun, I come bling horse."

His confidence relieved us of anxiety, and we had a very pleasant day of it, digesting our bountiful meal of salmon and potatoes, and mending up our clothing. We were now pretty ragged and very brown, but in excellent health.

Late in the afternoon a gang of road-cutters (who had been sent out by the towns interested in the route) came into town from Hazleton, and I had a talk with the boss, a very decent fellow, who gave a grim report of the trail beyond. He said: "Nobody knows anything about that trail. Jim Deacon, the head-man of our party when we left Hazleton, was only about seventy miles out, and cutting fallen timber like a man chopping cord wood, and sending back for more help. We are now going back to bridge and corduroy the places we had no time to fix as we came."

Morricetown was a superb spot, and Burton was much inclined to stay right there and prospect the near-by mountains. So far as a mere casual observer could determine, this country offers every inducement to prospectors. It is possible to grow potatoes, hay, and oats, together with various small fruits, in this valley, and if gold should ever be discovered in the rushing mountain streams, it would be easy to sustain a camp and feed it well.

Long before sunset an Indian came up to us and smilingly said, " You hoss — come." And a few minutes later the young ty-ee came riding into town leading " Major Grunt," well as ever, but a little sullen. He had taken the back trail till he came to a narrow and insecure bridge. There he had turned up the stream, going deeper and deeper into the " stick," as the Siwash called the forest. I paid the reward gladly, and Major took his place among the other horses with no sign of joy.

DO YOU FEAR THE WIND?

Do you fear the force of the wind,
The slash of the rain?
Go face them and fight them,
Be savage again.
Go hungry and cold like the wolf,
    Go wade like the crane.
The palms of your hands will thicken,
The skin of your cheek will tan,
You'll grow ragged and weary and swarthy,
    But you'll walk like a man!

CHAPTER XI

HAZLETON. MIDWAY ON THE TRAIL

WE were now but thirty miles from Hazleton, where our second bill of supplies was waiting for us, and we were eager to push on. Taking the advice of the road-gang we crossed the frail suspension bridge (which the Indians had most ingeniously constructed out of logs and pieces of old telegraph wire) and started down the west side of the river. Every ravine was filled by mountain streams' foam — white with speed.

We descended all day and the weather grew more and more summer-like each mile. Ripe strawberries lured us from the warm banks. For the first time we came upon great groves of red cedar under which the trail ran very muddy and very slippery by reason of the hard roots of the cedars which never decay. Creeks that seemed to me a good field for placer mining came down from the left, but no one stopped to do more than pan a little gravel from a cut bank or a bar.

At about two o'clock of the second day we came to the Indian village of Hagellgate, which stands on the high bank overhanging the roaring river just before it empties into the Skeena. Here we got news of the tramp who had fallen in exhaustion and was being cared for by the Indians.

Descending swiftly we came to the bank of the river, which was wide, tremendously swift and deep and cold. Rival Indian ferry companies bid for our custom, each man extolling his boat at the expense of the " old canoe — no good " of his rivals.

The canoes were like those to be seen all along the coast, that is to say they had been hollowed from cotton-wood or pine trees and afterward steamed and spread by means of hot water to meet the maker's idea of the proper line of grace and speed. They were really beautiful and sat the water almost as gracefully as the birch-bark canoe of the Chippewas. At each end they rose into a sort of neck, which terminated often in a head carved to resemble a deer or some fabled animal. Some of them had white bands encircling the throat of this figurehead. Their paddles were short and broad, but light and strong.

These canoes are very seaworthy. As they were driven across the swift waters, they danced on the waves like leaves, and the boatmen bent to their oars with almost desperate energy and with most excited outcry.

Therein is expressed a mighty difference between the Siwash and the plains Indian. The Cheyenne, the Sioux, conceal effort, or fear, or enthusiasm. These little people chattered and whooped at each other like monkeys. Upon hearing them for the first time I imagined they were losing control of the boat. Judging from their accent they were shrieking phrases like these : —

" Quick, quick ! Dig in deep, Joe. Scratch now,

we're going down — whoop! Hay, now! All together — swing her, dog-gone ye — SWING HER!
Now straight — keep her straight! Can't ye see that
eddy? Whoop, whoop! Let out a link or two, you
spindle-armed child. Now *quick* or we're lost!"

While the other men seemed to reply in kind: "Oh,
rats, we're a makin' it. Head her toward that bush.
Don't get scared — trust me — I'll sling her ashore!"

A plains Indian, under similar circumstances, would
have strained every muscle till his bones cracked, before
permitting himself to show effort or excitement.

With all their confusion and chatter these little people
were always masters of the situation. They came out
right, no matter how savage the river, and the Bulkley
at this point was savage. Every drop of water was in
motion. It had no eddies, no slack water. Its momen-
tum was terrific. In crossing, the boatmen were obliged
to pole their canoes far up beyond the point at which
they meant to land; then, at the word, they swung into
the rushing current and pulled like fiends for the opposite shore. Their broad paddles dipped so rapidly they
resembled paddle-wheels. They kept the craft head-on
to the current, and did not attempt to charge the bank
directly, but swung-to broadside. In this way they led
our horses safely across, and came up smiling each time.

We found Hazleton to be a small village composed
mainly of Indians, with a big Hudson Bay post at its
centre. It was situated on a lovely green flat, but a few
feet above the Skeena, which was a majestic flood at this
point. There were some ten or fifteen outfits camped

in and about the village, resting and getting ready for the last half of the trail. Some of the would-be miners had come up the river in the little Hudson Bay steamer, which makes two or three trips a year, and were waiting for her next trip in order to go down again.

The town was filled with gloomy stories of the trail. No one knew its condition. In fact, it had not been travelled in seventeen years, except by the Indians on foot with their packs of furs. The road party was ahead, but toiling hard and hurrying to open a way for us.

As I now reread all the advance literature of this "prairie route," I perceived how skilfully every detail with regard to the last half of the trail had been slurred over. We had been led into a sort of sack, and the string was tied behind us.

The Hudson Bay agent said to me with perfect frankness, "There's no one in this village, except one or two Indians, who's ever been over the trail, or who can give you any information concerning it." He furthermore said, "A large number of these fellows who are starting in on this trip with their poor little cayuses will never reach the Stikeen River, and might better stop right here."

Feed was scarce here as everywhere, and we were forced to camp on the trail, some two miles above the town. In going to and from our tent we passed the Indian burial ground, which was very curious and interesting to me. It was a veritable little city of the dead, with streets of tiny, gayly painted little houses in which the silent and motionless ones had been laid in their last sleep. Each tomb was a shelter, a roof, and a tomb, and upon each the builder had lavished his highest skill in ornament. They were all vivid with paint and carving and lattice work. Each builder seemed trying to outdo his neighbor in making a cheerful habitation for his dead.

More curious still, in each house were the things which the dead had particularly loved. In one, a trunk contained all of a girl's much-prized clothing. A complete set of dishes was visible in another, while in a third I saw a wash-stand, bowl, pitcher, and mirror. There was something deeply touching to me in all this. They are so poor, their lives are so bare of comforts, that the consecration of these articles to the dead seemed a greater sacrifice than we, who count ourselves civilized, would make. Each chair, or table, or coat, or pair of shoes, costs many skins. The set of furniture meant many hard journeys in the cold, long days of trailing, trapping, and packing. The clothing had a high money value, yet it remained undisturbed. I saw one day a woman and two young girls halt to look timidly in at the window of a newly erected tomb, but only for a moment; and then, in a panic of fear and awe, they hurried away.

The days which followed were cold and gloomy, quite in keeping with the grim tales of the trail. Bodies of horses and mules, drowned in the attempt to cross the Skeena, were reported passing the wharf at the post. The wife of a retired Indian agent, who claimed to have been over the route many years ago, was interviewed by my partner. After saying that it was a terrible trail, she sententiously ended with these words, " Gentlemen, you may consider yourselves explorers."

I halted a very intelligent Indian who came riding by our camp. "How far to Teslin Lake?" I asked.

He mused. "Maybe so forty days, maybe so thirty days. Me think forty days."

"Good feed? Hy-u muck-a-muck?"

He looked at me in silence and his face grew a little graver. "Ha—lo muck-a-muck (no feed). Long time no glass. Hy-yu stick (woods). Hy-u river—all day swim."

Turning to Burton, I said, "Here we get at the truth of it. This man has no reason for lying. We need another horse, and we need fifty pounds more flour."

One by one the outfits behind us came dropping down into Hazleton in long trains of weary horses, some of them in very bad condition. Many of the gold-seekers determined to "quit." They sold their horses as best they could to the Indians (who were glad to buy them), and hired canoes to take them to the coast, intent to catch one of the steamers which ply to and fro between Skagway and Seattle.

But one by one, with tinkling bells and sharp outcry of drivers, other outfits passed us, cheerily calling: "Good luck! See you later," all bound for the "gold belt." Gloomy skies continued to fill the imaginative ones with forebodings, and all day they could be seen in groups about the village discussing ways and means. Quarrels broke out, and parties disbanded in discouragement and bitterness. The road to the golden river seemed to grow longer, and the precious sand more elusive, from day to day. Here at Hazleton, where they had hoped to reach a gold region, nothing was doing. Those who had visited the Kisgagash Mountains to the north were luke-warm in their reports, and no one felt like stopping to explore. The cry was, "On to Dawson."

Here in Hazleton I came upon the lame tramp. He had secured lodging in an empty shack and was being helped to food by some citizens in the town for whom he was doing a little work. Seeing me pass he called to me and began to inquire about the trail.

I read in the gleam of his eye an insane resolution to push forward. This I set about to check. "If you wish to commit suicide, start on this trail. The four hundred miles you have been over is a summer picnic excursion compared to that which is now to follow. My advice to you is to stay right where you are until the next Hudson Bay steamer comes by, then go to the captain and tell him just how you are situated, and ask him to carry you down to the coast. You are insane to think for a moment of attempting the four hundred miles of unknown trail between here and Glenora, especially without a cent in your pocket and no grub. You have no right to burden the other outfits with your needs."

This plain talk seemed to affect him and he looked aggrieved. "But what can I do? I have no money and no work."

I replied in effect: "Whatever you do, you can't afford to enter upon this trail, and you can't expect men who are already short of grub to feed and take care of you. There's a chance for you to work your way back to the coast on the Hudson Bay steamer. There's only starvation on the trail."

As I walked away he called after me, but I refused to return. I had the feeling in spite of all I had said that he would attempt to rustle a little grub and make his start on the trail. The whole goldseeking movement was, in a way, a craze; he was simply an extreme development of it.

It seemed necessary to break camp in order not to be eaten up by the Siwash dogs, whose peculiarities grew upon me daily. They were indeed strange beasts. They seemed to have no youth. I never saw them play; even the puppies were grave and sedate. They were never in a hurry and were not afraid. They got out of our way with the least possible exertion, looking meekly reproachful or snarling threateningly at us. They were ever watchful. No matter how apparently deep their slumber, they saw every falling crumb, they knew where we had hung our fish, and were ready as we turned our backs to make away with it. It was impossible to leave anything eatable for a single instant. Nothing but the sleight of hand of a conjurer could equal the mystery of their stealing.

After buying a fourth pack animal and reshoeing all our horses, we got our outfit into shape for the long, hard drive which lay before us. Every ounce of superfluous weight, every tool, every article not absolutely essential, was discarded and its place filled with food. We stripped ourselves like men going into battle, and on the third day lined up for Teslin Lake, six hundred miles to the north.

SIWASH GRAVES

Here in their tiny gayly painted homes
They sleep, these small dead people of the streams,
Their names unknown, their deeds forgot,
Their by-gone battles lost in dreams.
A few short days and we who laugh
Will be as still, will lie as low
As utterly in dark as they who rot
Here where the roses blow.
They fought, and loved, and toiled, and died,
As all men do, and all men must.
Of what avail ? we at the end
Fall quite as shapelessly to dust.

LINE UP, BRAVE BOYS

The packs are on, the cinches tight,
The patient horses wait,
Upon the grass the frost lies white,
The dawn is gray and late.
The leader's cry rings sharp and clear,
The campfires smoulder low;
Before us lies a shallow mere,
Beyond, the mountain snow.
> " *Line up, Billy, line up, boys,*
> *The east is gray with coming day,*
> *We must away, we cannot stay.*
> *Hy-o, hy-ak, brave boys !* "

Five hundred miles behind us lie,
As many more ahead,
Through mud and mire on mountains high
Our weary feet must tread.
So one by one, with loyal mind,
The horses swing to place,
The strong in lead, the weak behind,
In patient plodding grace.
> "*Hy-o, Buckskin, brave boy, Joe !*
> *The sun is high,*
> *The hid loons cry :*
> *Hy-ak — away !   Hy-o !*"

CHAPTER XII

CROSSING THE BIG DIVIDE

OUR stay at Hazleton in some measure removed the charm of the first view. The people were all so miserably poor, and the hosts of howling, hungry dogs made each day more distressing. The mountains remained splendid to the last; and as we made our start I looked back upon them with undiminished pleasure.

We pitched tent at night just below the ford, and opposite another Indian village in which a most mournful medicine song was going on, timed to the beating of drums. Dogs joined with the mourning of the people with cries of almost human anguish, to which the beat of the passionless drum added solemnity, and a sort of inexorable marching rhythm. It seemed to announce pestilence and flood, and made the beautiful earth a place of hunger and despair.

I was awakened in the early dawn by a singular cry repeated again and again on the farther side of the river. It seemed the voice of a woman uttering in wailing chant the most piercing agony of despairing love. It ceased as the sun arose and was heard no more. It was difficult to imagine such anguish in the bustle of the bright morning. It seemed as though it must have been an illusion — a dream of tragedy.

In the course of an hour's travel we came down to the sandy bottom of the river, whereon a half-dozen fine canoes were beached and waiting for us. The skilful natives set us across very easily, although it was the maddest and wildest of all the rivers we had yet seen. We crossed the main river just above the point at which the west fork enters. The horses were obliged to swim nearly half a mile, and some of them would not have reached the other shore had it not been for the Indians, who held their heads out of water from the sterns of the canoes, and so landed them safely on the bar just opposite the little village called Kispyox, which is also the Indian name of the west fork.

The trail made off up the eastern bank of this river, which was as charming as any stream ever imagined by a poet. The water was gray-green in color, swift and active. It looped away in most splendid curves, through opulent bottom lands, filled with wild roses, geranium plants, and berry blooms. Openings alternated with beautiful woodlands and grassy meadows, while over and beyond all rose the ever present mountains of the coast range, deep blue and snow-capped.

There was no strangeness in the flora — on the contrary, everything seemed familiar. Hazel bushes, poplars, pines, all growth was amazingly luxuriant. The trail was an Indian path, graceful and full of swinging curves. We had passed beyond the telegraph wire of the old trail.

Early in the afternoon we passed some five or six outfits camped on a beautiful grassy bank overlooking the river, and forming a most satisfying picture. The bells on the grazing horses were tinkling, and from sparkling fires, thin columns of smoke arose. Some of the young men were bathing, while others were washing their shirts in the sunny stream. There was a cheerful sound of whistling and rattling of tinware mingled with the sound of axes. Nothing could be more jocund, more typical, of the young men and the trail. It was one of the few pleasant camps of the long journey.

It was raining when we awoke, but before noon it cleared sufficiently to allow us to pack. We started at one, though the bushes were loaded with water, and had we not been well clothed in waterproof, we should have been drenched to the bone. We rode for four hours over a good trail, dodging wet branches in the pouring rain. It lightened at five, and we went into camp quite dry and comfortable.

We unpacked near an Indian ranch belonging to an old man and his wife, who came up at once to see us. They were good-looking, rugged old souls, like powerful Japanese. They could not speak Chinook, and we could not get much out of them. The old wife toted a monstrous big salmon up the hill to sell to us, but we had more fish than we could eat, and were forced to decline. There was a beautiful spring just back of the cabin, and the old man seemed to take pleasure in having us get our water from it. Neither did he object to our horses feeding about his house, where there was very excellent grass. It was a charming camping-place, wild flowers made the trail radiant even in the midst of rain. The wild roses grew in clumps of sprays as high as a horse's head.

Just before we determined to camp we had passed three or four outfits grouped together on the sward on the left bank of the river. As we rode by, one of the men had called to me saying: "You had better camp. It is thirty miles from here to feed." To this I had merely nodded, giving it little attention; but now as we sat around our campfire, Burton brought the matter up again: "If it is thirty miles to feed, we will have to get off early to-morrow morning and make as big a drive as we can, while the horses are fresh, and then make the latter part of the run on empty stomachs."

"Oh, I think they were just talking for our special benefit," I replied.

"No, they were in earnest. One of them came out to see me. He said he got his pointer from the mule train ahead of us. Feed is going to be very scarce, and the next run is fully thirty miles."

I insisted it could not be possible that we should go at once from the luxuriant pea-vine and bluejoint into a thirty-mile stretch of country where nothing grew. "There must be breaks in the forest where we can graze our horses."

It rained all night and in the morning it seemed as if it had settled into a week's downpour. However, we were quite comfortable with plenty of fresh salmon, and were not troubled except with the thought of the mud which would result from this rainstorm. We were falling steadily behind our schedule each day, but the horses were feeding and gaining strength — " And when we hit the trail, we will hit it hard," I said to Burton.

It was Sunday. The day was perfectly quiet and peaceful, like a rainy Sunday in the States. The old Indian below kept to his house all day, not visiting us. It is probable that he was a Catholic. The dogs came about us occasionally ; strange, solemn creatures that they are, they had the persistence of hunger and the silence of burglars.

It was raining when we awoke Monday morning, but we were now restless to get under way. We could not afford to spend another day waiting in the rain. It was gloomy business in camp, and at the first sign of lightening sky we packed up and started promptly at twelve o'clock.

That ride was the sternest we had yet experienced. It was like swimming in a sea of green water. The branches sloshed us with blinding raindrops. The mud spurted under our horses' hoofs, the sky was gray and drizzled moisture, and as we rose we plunged into ever deepening forests. We left behind us all hazel bushes, alders, wild roses, and grasses. Moss was on every leaf and stump : the forest became savage, sinister and silent, not a living thing but ourselves moved or uttered voice.

This world grew oppressive with its unbroken clear greens, its dripping branches, its rotting trees ; its snake-like roots half buried in the earth convinced me that our warning was well-born. At last we came into upper heights where no blade of grass grew, and we pushed on desperately, on and on, hour after hour. We began to suffer with the horses, being hungry and cold ourselves. We plunged into bottomless mudholes, slid down slippery slopes of slate, and leaped innumerable fallen logs of fir. The sky had no more pity than the mossy ground and the desolate forest. It was a mocking land, a land of green things, but not a blade of grass : only austere trees and noxious weeds.

During the day we met an old man so loaded down I could not tell whether he was man, woman, or beast. A sort of cap or wide cloth band went across his head, concealing his forehead. His huge pack loomed over his shoulders, and as he walked, using two paddles as canes, he seemed some anomalous four-footed beast of burden.

As he saw us he threw off his pack to rest and stood erect, a sturdy man of sixty, with short bristling hair framing a kindly resolute face. He was very light-hearted. He shook hands with me, saying, " Kla-how-ya," in answer to my, " Kla-how-ya six," which is to say, " How are you, friend ? " He smiled, pointed to his pack, and said, " Hy-u skin." His season had been successful and he was going now to sell his catch. A couple of dogs just behind carried each twenty pounds on their backs. We were eating lunch, and I invited him to sit and eat. He took a seat and began to parcel out the food in two piles.

" He has a companion coming," I said to my partner. In a few moments a boy of fourteen or fifteen came up, carrying a pack that would test the strength of a powerful white man. He, too, threw off his load and at a word from the old man took a seat at the table. They shared exactly alike. It was evident that they were father and son.

A few miles farther on we met another family, two men, a woman, a boy, and six dogs, all laden in proportion. They were all handsomer than the Siwashes of the Fraser River. They came from the head-waters of the Nasse, they said. They could speak but little Chinook and no English at all. When I asked in Chinook, "How far is it to feed for our horses?" the woman looked first at our thin animals, then at us, and shook her head sorrowfully; then lifting her hands in the most dramatic gesture she half whispered, "Si-ah, si-ah!" That is to say, "Far, very far!"

Both these old people seemed very kind to their dogs, which were fat and sleek and not related to those I had seen in Hazleton. When the old man spoke to them, his voice was gentle and encouraging. At the word they all took up the line of march and went off down the hill toward the Hudson Bay store, there to remain during the summer. We pushed on, convinced by the old woman's manner that our long trail was to be a gloomy one.

Night began to settle over us at last, adding the final touches of uncertainty and horror to the gloom. We pushed on with necessary cruelty, forcing the tired horses to their utmost, searching every ravine and every slope for a feed; but only ferns and strange green poi-

I

sonous plants could be seen. We were angling up the side of the great ridge which separated the west fork of the Skeena River from the middle fork. It was evident that we must cross this high divide and descend into the valley of the middle fork before we could hope to feed our horses.

However, just as darkness was beginning to come on, we came to an almost impassable slough in the trail, where a small stream descended into a little flat marsh and morass. This had been used as a camping-place by others, and we decided to camp, because to travel, even in the twilight, was dangerous to life and limb.

It was a gloomy and depressing place to spend the night. There was scarcely level ground enough to receive our camp. The wood was soggy and green. In order to reach the marsh we were forced to lead our horses one by one through a dangerous mudhole, and once through this they entered upon a quaking bog, out of which grew tufts of grass which had been gnawed to the roots by the animals which had preceded them; only a rank bottom of dead leaves of last year's growth was left for our tired horses. I was deeply anxious for fear they would crowd into the central bog in their efforts to reach the uncropped green blades which grew out of reach in the edge of the water. They were ravenous with hunger after eight hours of hard labor.

Our clothing was wet to the inner threads, and we were tired and muddy also, but our thoughts were on the horses rather than upon ourselves. We soon had a fire going and some hot supper, and by ten o'clock were stretched out in our beds for the night.

I have never in my life experienced a gloomier or more distressing camp on the trail. My bed was dry and warm, but I could not forget our tired horses grubbing about in the chilly night on that desolate marsh.

A CHILD OF THE SUN

Give me the sun and the sky,
The wide sky.   Let it blaze with light,
Let it burn with heat — I care not.
The sun is the blood of my heart,
The wind of the plain my breath.
No woodsman am I.   My eyes are set
For the wide low lines.   The level rim
Of the prairie land is mine.
The semi-gloom of the pointed firs,
The sleeping darks of the mountain spruce,
Are prison and poison to such as I.
In the forest I long for the rose of the plain,
In the dark of the firs I die.

O to lie in long grasses!
O to dream of the plain!
Where the west wind sings as it passes
A weird and unceasing refrain;
Where the rank grass wallows and tosses,
And the plains' ring dazzles the eye;
Where hardly a silver cloud bosses
The flashing steel arch of the sky.

To watch the gay gulls as they flutter
Like snowflakes and fall down the sky,
To swoop in the deeps of the hollows,
Where the crow's-foot tosses awry;
And gnats in the lee of the thickets
Are swirling like waltzers in glee
To the harsh, shrill creak of the crickets
And the song of the lark and the bee.

O far-off plains of my west land!
O lands of winds and the free,
Swift deer — my mist-clad plain!
From my bed in the heart of the forest,
From the clasp and the girdle of pain
Your light through my darkness passes;
To your meadows in dreaming I fly
To plunge in the deeps of your grasses,
To bask in the light of your sky!

CHAPTER XIII

THE SILENT FORESTS OF THE DREAD SKEENA

WE were awake early and our first thought was of our horses. They were quite safe and cropping away on the dry stalks with patient diligence. We saddled up and pushed on, for food was to be had only in the valley, whose blue and white walls we could see far ahead of us. After nearly six hours' travel we came out of the forest, out into the valley of the middle fork of the Skeena, into sunlight and grass in abundance, where we camped till the following morning, giving the horses time to recuperate.

We were done with smiling valleys — that I now perceived. We were coming nearer to the sub-arctic country, grim and desolate. The view was magnificent, but the land seemed empty and silent except of mosquitoes, of which there were uncounted millions. On our right just across the river rose the white peaks of the Kisgagash Mountains. Snow was still lying in the gullies only a few rods above us.

The horses fed right royally and soon forgot the dearth of the big divide. As we were saddling up to move the following morning, several outfits came trailing down into the valley, glad as we had been of the splendid field of grass. They were led by a grizzled old American, who cursed the country with fine fervor.

"I can stand any kind of a country," said he, "except one where there's no feed. And as near's I can find out we're in fer hell's own time fer feed till we reach them prairies they tell about."

After leaving this flat, we had the Kuldo (a swift and powerful river) to cross, but we found an old Indian and a girl camped on the opposite side waiting for us. The daughter, a comely child about sixteen years of age, wore a calico dress and "store" shoes. She was a self-contained little creature, and clearly in command of the boat, and very efficient. It was no child's play to put the light canoe across such a stream, but the old man, with much shouting and under command of the girl, succeeded in crossing six times, carrying us and our baggage. As we were being put across for the last time it became necessary for some one to pull the canoe through the shallow water, and the little girl, without hesitation, leaped out regardless of new shoes, and tugged at the rope while the old man poled at the stern, and so we were landed.

As a recognition of her resolution I presented her with a dollar, which I tried to make her understand was her own, and not to be given to her father. Up to that moment she had been very shy and rather sullen, but my present seemed to change her opinion of us, and she became more genial at once. She was short and sturdy, and her little footsteps in the trail were strangely suggestive of civilization.

After leaving the river we rose sharply for about three miles. This brought us to the first notice on the trail which was signed by the road-gang, an ambiguous scrawl to the effect that feed was to be very scarce for a long, long way, and that we should feed our horses before going forward. The mystery of the sign lay in the fact that no feed was in sight, and if it referred back to the flat, then it was in the nature of an Irish bull.

There was a fork in the trail here, and another notice informed us that the trail to the right ran to the Indian village of Kuldo. Rain threatened, and as it was late and no feed promised, I determined to camp. Turning to the right down a tremendously steep path (the horses sliding on their haunches), we came to an old Indian fishing village built on a green shelf high above the roaring water of the Skeena.

The people all came rushing out to see us, curious but very hospitable. Some of the children began plucking grasses for the horses, but being unaccustomed to animals of any kind, not one would approach within reach of them. I tried, by patting Ladrone and putting his head over my shoulder, to show them how gentle he was, but they only smiled and laughed as much as to say, "Yes, that is all right for *you*, but we are afraid." They were all very good-looking, smiling folk, but poorly dressed. They seemed eager to show us where the best grass grew, demanded nothing of us, begged nothing, and did not attempt to overcharge us. There were some eight or ten families in the cañon, and their houses were wretched shacks, mere lodges of slabs with vents in the peak. So far as they could, they conformed to the ways of white men.

Here they dwell by this rushing river in the midst of a gloomy and trackless forest, far removed from any other people of any sort. They were but a handful of human souls. As they spoke little Chinook and almost no English, it was difficult to converse with them. They had lost the sign language or seemed not to use it. Their village was built here because the cañon below offered a capital place for fishing and trapping, and the principal duty of the men was to watch the salmon trap dancing far below. For the rest they hunt wild animals and sell furs to the Hudson Bay Company at Hazleton, which is their metropolis.

They led us to the edge of the village and showed us where the road-gang had set their tent, and we soon had a fire going in our little stove, which was the amazement and delight of a circle of men, women, and children, but they were not intrusive and asked for nothing.

Later in the evening the old man and the girl who had helped to ferry us across the Kuldo came down the hill and joined the circle of our visitors.

She smiled as we greeted her and so did the father, who assured me he was the ty-ee (boss) of the village, which he seemed to be.

After our supper we distributed some fruit among the children, and among the old women some hot coffee with sugar, which was a keen delight to them. Our desire to be friendly was deeply appreciated by these poor people, and our wish to do them good was greater than our means. The way was long before us and we could not afford to give away our supplies. How they live in winter I cannot understand; probably they go down the river to Hazleton.

I began to dread the dark green dripping firs which seemed to encompass us like some vast army. They chilled me, oppressed me. Moreover, I was lame in every joint from the toil of crossing rivers, climbing steep hills, and dragging at cinches. I had walked down every hill and in most cases on the sharp upward slopes in order to relieve Ladrone of my weight.

As we climbed back to our muddy path next day, we were filled with dark forebodings of the days to come. We climbed all day, keeping the bench high above the river. The land continued silent. It was a wilderness of firs and spruce pines. It was like a forest of bronze. Nothing but a few rose bushes and some leek-like plants rose from the mossy floor, on which the sun fell, weak and pale, in rare places. No beast or bird uttered sound save a fishing eagle swinging through the cañon above the roaring water.

In the gloom the voice of the stream became a raucous roar. On every side cold and white and pitiless the snowy peaks lifted above the serrate rim of the forest.

Life was scant here. In all the mighty spread of forest between the continental divide on the east and the coast range at the west there are few living things, and these few necessarily centre in the warm openings on the banks of the streams where the sunlight falls or in the high valleys above the firs. There are no serpents and no insects.

As we mounted day by day we crossed dozens of swift little streams cold and gray with silt. Our rate of speed was very low. One of our horses became very weak and ill, evidently poisoned, and we were forced to stop often to rest him. All the horses were weakening day by day.

Toward the middle of the third day, after crossing a stream which came from the left, the trail turned as if to leave the Skeena behind. We were mighty well pleased and climbed sharply and with great care of our horses till we reached a little meadow at the summit, very tired and disheartened, for the view showed only other peaks and endless waves of spruce and fir. We rode on under drizzling skies and dripping trees. There was little sunshine and long lines of heavily weighted gray clouds came crawling up the valley from the sea to break in cold rain over the summits.

The horses again grew hungry and weak, and it was necessary to use great care in crossing the streams. We were lame and sore with the toil of the day, and what was more depressing found ourselves once more upon the banks of the Skeena, where only an occasional bunch of bluejoint could be found. The constant strain of watching the horses and guiding them through the mud began to tell on us both. There was now no moment of ease, no hour of enjoyment. We had set ourselves grimly to the task of bringing our horses through alive. We no longer rode, we toiled in silence, leading our saddle-horses on which we had packed a part of our outfit to relieve the sick and starving packhorses.

On the fourth day we took a westward shoot from the river, and following the course of a small stream again climbed heavily up the slope. Our horses were now so weak we could only climb a few rods at a time without rest. But at last, just as night began to fall, we came upon a splendid patch of bluejoint, knee-deep and rich. It was high on the mountain side, on a slope so steep that the horses could not lie down, so steep that it was almost impossible to set our tent. We could not persuade ourselves to pass it, however, and so made the best of it. Everywhere we could see white mountains, to the south, to the west, to the east.

"Now we have left the Skeena Valley," said Burton.

"Yes, we have seen the last of the Skeena," I replied, "and I'm glad of it. I never want to see that gray-green flood again."

A part of the time that evening we spent in picking the thorns of devil's-club out of our hands. This strange plant I had not seen before, and do not care to see it again. In plunging through the mudholes we spasmodically clutched these spiny things. Ladrone nipped steadily at the bunch of leaves which grew at the top of the twisted stalk. Again we plunged down into the cold green forest, following a stream whose current ran to the northeast. This brought us once again to the bank of the dreaded Skeena. The trail was "punishing," and the horses plunged and lunged all day through the mud, over logs, stones, and roots.

Our nerves quivered with the torture of piloting our mistrusted desperate horses through these awful pitfalls. We were still in the region of ferns and devil's-club.

We allowed no feed to escape us. At any hour of the day, whenever we found a bunch of grass, no matter if it were not bigger than a broom, we stopped for the horses to graze it and so we kept them on their feet.

At five o'clock in the afternoon we climbed to a low, marshy lake where an Indian hunter was camped. He said we would find feed on another lake some miles up, and we pushed on, wallowing through mud and water of innumerable streams, each moment in danger of leaving a horse behind. I walked nearly all day, for it was torture to me as well as to Ladrone to ride him over such a trail. Three of our horses now showed signs of poisoning, two of them walked with a sprawling action of the fore legs, their eyes big and glassy. One was too weak to carry anything more than his pack-saddle, and our going had a sort of sullen desperation in it. Our camps were on the muddy ground, without comfort or convenience.

Next morning, as I swung into the saddle and started at the head of my train, Ladrone threw out his nose with a sharp indrawn squeal of pain. At first I paid little attention to it, but it came again — and then I noticed a weakness in his limbs. I dismounted and examined him carefully. He, too, was poisoned and attacked by spasms. It was a sorrowful thing to see my proud gray reduced to this condition.   His eyes were dilated and glassy and his joints were weak.   We could not stop, we could not wait, we must push on to feed and open ground; and so leading him carefully I resumed our slow march.

But at last, just when it seemed as though we could not go any farther with our suffering animals, we came out of the poisonous forest upon a broad grassy bottom where a stream was flowing to the northwest.   We raised a shout of joy, for it seemed this must be a branch of the Nasse.   If so, we were surely out of the clutches of the Skeena.   This bottom was the first dry and level ground we had seen since leaving the west fork, and the sun shone.   " Old man, the worst of our trail is over," I shouted to my partner.   " The land looks more open to the north.   We're coming to that plateau they told us of."

Oh, how sweet, fine, and sunny the short dry grass seemed to us after our long toilsome stay in the sub-aqueous gloom of the Skeena forests !   We seemed about to return to the birds and the flowers.

Ladrone was very ill, but I fed him some salt mixed with lard, and after a doze in the sun he began to nibble grass with the others, and at last stretched out on the warm dry sward to let the glorious sun soak into his blood.   It was a joyous thing to us to see the faithful ones revelling in the healing sunlight, their stomachs filled at last with sweet rich forage.   We were dirty, ragged, and lame, and our hands were calloused and seamed with dirt, but we were strong and hearty.

We were high in the mountains here. Those little marshy lakes and slow streams showed that we were on a divide, and to our minds could be no other than the head-waters of the Nasse, which has a watershed of its own to the sea. We believed the worst of our trip to be over.

THE FAITHFUL BRONCOS

They go to certain death — to freeze,
To grope their way through blinding snow,
To starve beneath the northern trees —
Their curse on us who made them go!
They trust and we betray the trust;
They humbly look to us for keep.
The rifle crumbles them to dust,
And we — have hardly grace to weep
As they line up to die.

THE WHISTLING MARMOT

On mountains cold and bold and high,
Where only golden eagles fly,
He builds his home against the sky.

Above the clouds he sits and whines,
The morning sun about him shines;
Rivers loop below in shining lines.

No wolf or cat may find him there,
That winged corsair of the air,
The eagle, is his only care.

He sees the pink snows slide away,
He sees his little ones at play,
And peace fills out each summer day.

In winter, safe within his nest,
He eats his winter store with zest,
And takes his young ones to his breast.

CHAPTER XIV

THE GREAT STIKEEN DIVIDE

AT about eight o'clock the next morning, as we were about to line up for our journey, two men came romping down the trail, carrying packs on their backs and taking long strides. They were "hitting the high places in the scenery," and seemed to be entirely absorbed in the work. I hailed them and they turned out to be two young men from Duluth, Minnesota. They were without hats, very brown, very hairy, and very much disgusted with the country.

For an hour we discussed the situation. They were the first white men we had met on the entire journey, almost the only returning footsteps, and were able to give us a little information of the trail, but only for a distance of about forty miles; beyond this they had not ventured.

"We left our outfits back here on a little lake — maybe you saw our Indian guide — and struck out ahead to see if we could find those splendid prairies they were telling us about, where the caribou and the moose were so thick you couldn't miss 'em. We've been forty miles up the trail. It's all a climb, and the very worst yet. You'll come finally to a high snowy divide with nothing but mountains on every side. There *is* no prairie; it's all a lie, and we're going back to Hazleton to go around by way of Skagway. Have you any idea where we are?"

"Why, certainly; we're in British Columbia."

"But where?   On what stream?"

"Oh, that is a detail," I replied.   "I consider the little camp on which we are camped one of the head-waters of the Nasse; but we're not on the Telegraph Trail at all.   We're more nearly in line with the old Dease Lake Trail."

"Why is it, do you suppose, that the road-gang ahead of us haven't left a single sign, not even a word as to where we are?"

"Maybe they can't write," said my partner.

"Perhaps they don't know where they are at, themselves," said I.

"Well, that's exactly the way it looks to me."

"Are there any outfits ahead of us?"

"Yes, old Bob Borlan's about two days up the slope with his train of mules, working like a slave to get through.   They're all getting short of grub and losing a good many horses.   You'll have to work your way through with great care, or you'll lose a horse or two in getting from here to the divide."

"Well, this won't do.   So-long, boys," said one of the young fellows, and they started off with immense vigor, followed by their handsome dogs, and we lined up once more with stern faces, knowing now that a terrible trail for at least one hundred miles was before us.   There was no thought of retreat, however. We had set our feet to this journey, and we determined to go.

After a few hours' travel we came upon the grassy shore of another little lake, where the bells of several outfits were tinkling merrily. On the bank of a swift little river setting out of the lake, a couple of tents stood, and shirts were flapping from the limbs of near-by willows. The owners were " The Man from Chihuahua," his partner, the blacksmith, and the two young men from Manchester, New Hampshire, who had started from Ashcroft as markedly tenderfoot as any men could be. They had been lambasted and worried into perfect efficiency as packers and trailers, and were entitled to respect — even the respect of " The Man from Chihuahua."

They greeted us with jovial outcry.

" Hullo, strangers ! Where ye think you're goin' ? "

" Goin' crazy," replied Burton.

" You look it," said Bill.

" By God, we was all sure crazy when we started on this damn trail," remarked the old man. He was in bad humor on account of his horses, two of which were suffering from poisoning. When anything touched his horses, he was " plum irritable."

He came up to me very soberly. " Have you any idee where we're at ? "

" Yes — we're on the head-waters of the Nasse."

" Are we on the Telegraph Trail ? "

" No ; as near as I can make out we're away to the right of the telegraph crossing."

Thereupon we compared maps. "It's mighty little use to look at maps — they're all drew by guess — an' — by God, anyway," said the old fellow, as he ran his grimy forefinger over the red line which represented the trail. "We've been a shoutin' hell words ever since we crossed the Skeeny — I figure it we're on the old Dease Lake Trail."

To this we all agreed at last, but our course thereafter was by no means clear.

"If we took the old Dease Lake Trail we're three hundred miles from Telegraph Creek yit — an' some-body's goin' to be hungry before we get in," said the old trailer. "I'd like to camp here for a few days and feed up my horses, but it ain't safe — we got 'o keep movin'. We've been on this damn trail long enough, and besides grub is gittin' lighter all the time."

"What do you think of the trail?" asked Burton.

"I've been on the trail all my life," he replied, "an' I never was in such a pizen, empty no-count country in my life. Wasn't that big divide hell? Did ye ever see the beat of that fer a barren? No more grass than a cellar. Might as well camp in a cistern. I wish I could lay hands on the feller that called this ' The Prairie Route ' — they'd sure be a dog-fight right here."

The old man expressed the feeling of those of us who were too shy and delicate of speech to do it justice, and we led him on to most satisfying blasphemy of the land and the road-gang.

"Yes, there's that road-gang sent out to put this trail into shape — what have they done? You'd think they couldn't read or write — not a word to help us out."

Partner and I remained in camp all the afternoon and all the next day, although our travelling companions packed up and moved out the next morning. We felt the need of a day's freedom from worry, and our horses needed feed and sunshine.

Oh, the splendor of the sun, the fresh green grass, the rippling water of the river, the beautiful lake! And what joy it was to see our horses feed and sleep. They looked distressingly thin and poor without their saddles. Ladrone was still weak in the ankle joints and the arch had gone out of his neck, while faithful Bill, who never murmured or complained, had a glassy stare in his eyes, the lingering effects of poisoning. The wind rose in the afternoon, bringing to us a sound of moaning tree-tops, and somehow it seemed to be an augury of better things — seemed to prophesy a fairer and dryer country to the north of us. The singing of the leaves went to my heart with a hint of home, and I remembered with a start how absolutely windless the sullen forest of the Skeena had been.

Near by a dam was built across the river, and a fishing trap made out of willows was set in the current. Piles of caribou hair showed that the Indians found game in the autumn. We took time to explore some old fishing huts filled with curious things, — skins, toboggans, dog-collars, cedar ropes, and many other traps of small value to anybody. Most curious of all we found some flint-lock muskets made exactly on the models of one hundred years ago, but dated 1883! It seemed impossible that guns of such ancient models should be manufactured up to the present date; but there they were all carefully marked "London, 1883."

It was a long day of rest and regeneration. We took a bath in the clear, cold waters of the stream, washed our clothing and hung it up to dry, beat the mud out of our towels, and so made ready for the onward march. We should have stayed longer, but the ebbing away of our grub pile made us apprehensive. To return was impossible.

THE CLOUDS

Circling the mountains the gray clouds go
Heavy with storms as a mother with child,
Seeking release from their burden of snow
With calm slow motion they cross the wild —
Stately and sombre, they catch and cling
To the barren crags of the peaks in the west,
Weary with waiting, and mad for rest.

THE GREAT STIKEEN DIVIDE

A land of mountains based in hills of fir,
Empty, lone, and cold.   A land of streams
Whose roaring voices drown the whirr
Of aspen leaves, and fill the heart with dreams
Of dearth and death.   The peaks are stern and white
The skies above are grim and gray,
And the rivers cleave their sounding way
Through endless forests dark as night,
Toward the ocean's far-off line of spray.

CHAPTER XV

IN THE COLD GREEN MOUNTAINS

THE Nasse River, like the Skeena and the Stikeen, rises in the interior mountains, and flows in a south-westerly direction, breaking through the coast range into the Pacific Ocean, not far from the mouth of the Stikeen.

It is a much smaller stream than the Skeena, which is, moreover, immensely larger than the maps show. We believed we were about to pass from the water-shed of the Nasse to the east fork of the Iskoot, on which those far-shining prairies were said to lie, with their flowery meadows rippling under the west wind. If we could only reach that mystical plateau, our horses would be safe from all disease.

We crossed the Cheweax, a branch of the Nasse, and after climbing briskly to the northeast along the main branch we swung around over a high wooded hog-back, and made off up the valley along the north and lesser fork. We climbed all day, both of us walking, leading our horses, with all our goods distributed with great care over the six horses. It was a beautiful day overhead — that was the only compensation. We were sweaty, eaten by flies and mosquitoes, and covered with mud.

All day we sprawled over roots, rocks, and logs, plunging into bogholes and slopping along in the running water, which in places had turned the trail into an aqueduct. The men from Duluth had told no lie.

After crawling upward for nearly eight hours we came upon a little patch of bluejoint, on the high side of the hill, and there camped in the gloom of the mossy and poisonous forest. By hard and persistent work we ticked off nearly fifteen miles, and judging from the stream, which grew ever swifter, we should come to a divide in the course of fifteen or twenty miles.

The horses being packed light went along fairly well, although it was a constant struggle to get them to go through the mud. Old Ladrone walking behind me groaned with dismay every time we came to one of those terrible sloughs. He seemed to plead with me, "Oh, my master, don't send me into that dreadful hole!"

But there was no other way. It must be done, and so Burton's sharp cry would ring out behind and our little train would go in one after the other, plunging, splashing, groaning, struggling through. Ladrone, seeing me walk a log by the side of the trail, would sometimes follow me as deftly as a cat. He seemed to think his right to avoid the mud as good as mine. But as there was always danger of his slipping off and injuring himself, I forced him to wallow in the mud, which was as distressing to me as to him.

The next day we started with the determination to reach the divide. "There is no hope of grass so long as we remain in this forest," said Burton. "We must get above timber where the sun shines to get any feed for our horses. It is cruel, but we must push them to-day just as long as they can stand up, or until we reach the grass."

Nothing seemed to appall or disturb my partner; he was always ready to proceed, his voice ringing out with inflexible resolution.

It was one of the most laborious days of all our hard journey. Hour after hour we climbed steadily up beside the roaring gray-white little stream, up toward the far-shining snowfields, which blazed back the sun like mirrors. The trees grew smaller, the river bed seemed to approach us until we slumped along in the running water. At last we burst out into the light above timber line. Around us porcupines galloped, and whistling marmots signalled with shrill vehemence. We were weak with fatigue and wet with icy water to the knees, but we pushed on doggedly until we came to a little mound of short, delicious green grass from which the snow had melted. On this we stopped to let the horses graze. The view was magnificent, and something wild and splendid came on the wind over the snowy peaks and smooth grassy mounds.

We were now in the region of great snowfields, under which roared swift streams from still higher altitudes. There were thousands of marmots, which seemed to utter the most intense astonishment at the inexplicable coming of these strange creatures. The snow in the gullies had a curious bloody line which I could not account for. A little bird high up here uttered a sweet little whistle, so sad, so full of pleading, it almost brought tears to my eyes. In form it resembled a horned lark, but was smaller and kept very close to the ground.

We reached the summit at sunset, there to find only other mountains and other enormous gulches leading downward into far blue cañons. It was the wildest land I have ever seen. A country unmapped, unsurveyed, and unprospected. A region which had known only an occasional Indian hunter or trapper with his load of furs on his way down to the river and his canoe. Desolate, without life, green and white and flashing illimitably, the gray old peaks aligned themselves rank on rank until lost in the mists of still wilder regions.

From this high point we could see our friends, the Manchester boys, on the north slope two or three miles below us at timber line. Weak in the knees, cold and wet and hungry as we were, we determined to push down the trail over the snowfields, down to grass and water. Not much more than forty minutes later we came out upon a comparatively level spot of earth where grass was fairly good, and where the wind-twisted stunted pines grew in clumps large enough to furnish wood for our fires and a pole for our tent. The land was meshed with roaring rills of melting snow, and all around went on the incessant signalling of the marmots — the only cheerful sound in all the wide green land.

We had made about twenty-three miles that day, notwithstanding tremendous steeps and endless mudholes mid-leg deep. It was the greatest test of endurance of our trip.

We had the good luck to scare up a ptarmigan (a sort of piebald mountain grouse), and though nearly fainting with hunger, we held ourselves in check until we had that bird roasted to a turn. I shall never experience greater relief or sweeter relaxation of rest than that I felt as I stretched out in my down-sleeping bag for twelve hours' slumber.

I considered that we were about one hundred and ninety miles from Hazleton, and that this must certainly be the divide between the Skeena and the Stikeen. The Manchester boys reported finding some very good pieces of quartz on the hills, and they were all out with spade and pick prospecting, though it seemed to me they showed but very little enthusiasm in the search.

"I b'lieve there's gold here," said "Chihuahua," "but who's goin' to stay here and look fer it? In the first place, you couldn't work fer mor'n 'bout three months in the year, and it 'ud take ye the other nine months fer to git yer grub in. Them hills look to me to be mineralized, but I ain't honin' to camp here."

This seemed to be the general feeling of all the other prospectors, and I did not hear that any one else went so far even as to dig a hole.

As near as I could judge there seemed to be three varieties of "varmints" galloping around over the grassy slopes of this high country. The largest of these, a gray and brown creature with a tawny, bristling mane, I took to be a porcupine. Next in size were the giant whistlers, who sat up like old men and signalled, like one boy to another. And last and least, and more numerous than all, were the smaller "chucks" resembling prairie dogs. These animals together with the ptarmigan made up the inhabitants of these lofty slopes.

I searched every green place on the mountains far and near with my field-glasses, but saw no sheep, caribou, or moose, although one or two were reported to have been killed by others on the trail. The ptarmigan lived in the matted patches of willow. There were a great many of them, and they helped out our monotonous diet very opportunely. They moved about in pairs, the cock very loyal to the hen in time of danger; but not even this loyalty could save him. Hunger such as ours considered itself very humane in stopping short of the slaughter of the mother bird. The cock was easily distinguished by reason of his party-colored plumage and his pink eyes.

We spent the next forenoon in camp to let our horses feed up, and incidentally to rest our own weary bones. All the forenoon great, gray clouds crushed against the divide behind us, flinging themselves in rage against the rocks like hungry vultures baffled in their chase. We exulted over their impotence. "We are done with you, you storms of the Skeena — we're out of your reach at last!"

We were confirmed in this belief as we rode down the trail, which was fairly pleasant except for short periods, when the clouds leaped the snowy walls behind and scattered drizzles of rain over us. Later the clouds thickened, the sky became completely overcast, and my exultation changed to dismay, and we camped at night as desolate as ever, in the rain, and by the side of a little marsh on which the horses could feed only by wading fetlock deep in the water. We were wet to the skin, and muddy and tired.

I could no longer deceive myself. Our journey had become a grim race with the wolf. Our food grew each day scantier, and we were forced to move each day and every day, no matter what the sky or trail might be. Going over our food carefully that night, we calculated that we had enough to last us ten days, and if we were within one hundred and fifty miles of the Skeena, and if no accident befell us, we would be able to pull in without great suffering.

But accidents on the trail are common. It is so easy to lose a couple of horses, we were liable to delay and to accident, and the chances were against us rather than in our favor. It seemed as though the trail would never mend. We were dropping rapidly down through dwarf pines, down into endless forests of gloom again. We had splashed, slipped, and tumbled down the trail to this point with three horses weak and sick. The rain had increased, and all the brightness of the morning on the high mountain had passed away. For hours we had walked without a word except to our horses, and now night was falling in thick, cold rain. As I plodded along I saw in vision and with great longing the plains, whose heat and light seemed paradise by contrast.

The next day was the Fourth of July, and such a day! It rained all the forenoon, cold, persistent, drizzling rain. We hung around the campfire waiting for

L

some let-up to the incessant downpour. We discussed the situation. I said : " Now, if the stream in the cañon below us runs to the left, it will be the east fork of the Iscoot, and we will then be within about one hundred miles of Glenora. If it runs to the right, Heaven only knows where we are."

The horses, chilled with the rain, came off the sloppy marsh to stand under the trees, and old Ladrone edged close to the big fire to share its warmth. This caused us to bring in the other horses and put them close to the fire under the big branches of the fir tree. It was deeply pathetic to watch the poor worn animals, all life and spirit gone out of them, standing about the fire with drooping heads and half-closed eyes. Perhaps they dreamed, like us, of the beautiful, warm, grassy hills of the south.

THE UTE LOVER

Beneath the burning brazen sky,
The yellowed tepes stand.
Not far away a singing
Sets through the sand.
Within the shadow of a lonely elm tree
The tired ponies keep.
The wild land, throbbing with the sun's hot magic,
Is rapt as sleep.

From out a clump of scanty willows
A low wail floats.
The endless repetition of a lover's
Melancholy notes;
So sad, so sweet, so elemental,
All lover's pain
Seems borne upon its sobbing cadence —
The love-song of the plain.
From frenzied cry forever falling,
To the wind's wild moan,
It seems the voice of anguish calling
Alone! alone!

Caught from the winds forever moaning
On the plain,
Wrought from the agonies of woman
In maternal pain,
It holds within its simple measure
All death of joy,
Breathed though it be by smiling maiden
Or lithe brown boy.

It hath this magic, sad though its cadence
And short refrain;
It helps the exiled people of the mountain
Endure the plain;
For when at night the stars aglitter
Defy the moon,
The maiden listens, leans to seek her lover
Where waters croon.

Flute on, O lithe and tuneful Utah,
Reply brown jade;
There are no other joys secure to either
Man or maid.
Soon you are old and heavy hearted,
Lost to mirth;
While on you lies the white man's gory
Greed of earth.

Strange that to me that burning desert
Seems so dear.
The endless sky and lonely mesa,
Flat and drear,
Calls me, calls me as the flute of Utah
Calls his mate —
This wild, sad, sunny, brazen country,
Hot as hate.

Again the glittering sky uplifts star-blazing;
Again the stream
From out the far-off snowy mountains
Sings through my dream;
And on the air I hear the flute-voice calling
The lover's croon,
And see the listening, longing maiden
Lit by the moon.

DEVIL'S CLUB

It is a sprawling, hateful thing,
Thorny and twisted like a snake,
Writhing to work a mischief, in the brake
It stands at menace, in its cling
Is danger and a venomed sting.
It grows on green and slimy slopes,
It is a thing of shades and slums,
For passing feet it wildly gropes,
And loops to catch all feet that run
Seeking a path to sky and sun.

IN THE COLD GREEN MOUNTAINS

In the cold green mountains where the savage torrents
    roared,
And the clouds were gray above us,
And the fishing eagle soared,
Where no grass waved, where no robins cried,
There our horses starved and died,
In the cold green mountains.

In the cold green mountains,
Nothing grew but moss and trees,
Water dripped and sludgy streamlets
Trapped our horses by the knees.
Where we slipped, slid, and lunged,
Mired down and wildly plunged
Toward the cold green mountains !

CHAPTER XVI

THE PASSING OF THE BEANS

AT noon, the rain slacking a little, we determined to pack up, and with such cheer as we could called out, " Line up, boys — line up ! " starting on our way down the trail.

After making about eight miles we came upon a number of outfits camped on the bank of the river.   As I rode along on my gray horse, for the trail there allowed me to ride, I passed a man seated gloomily at the mouth of his tent.   To him I called with an assumption of jocularity I did not feel, "Stranger, where are you bound for ? "

He replied, " The North Pole."

" Do you expect to get there ? "

" Sure," he replied.

Riding on I met others beside the trail, and all wore a similar look of almost sullen gravity.   They were not disposed to joke with me, and perceiving something to be wrong, I passed on without further remark.

When we came down to the bank of the stream, behold it ran to the right.   And I could have sat me down and blasphemed with the rest.   I now understood the gloom of the others.   *We were still in the valley of*

the inexorable Skeena.   It could be nothing else; this
tremendous stream running to our right could be no
other than the head-waters of that ferocious flood which
no surveyor has located.   It is immensely larger and
longer than any map shows.

We crossed the branch without much trouble, and
found some beautiful bluejoint-grass on the opposite
bank, into which we joyfully turned our horses.   When
they had filled their stomachs, we packed up and pushed
on about two miles, overtaking the Manchester boys on
the side-hill in a tract of dead, burned-out timber, a
cheerless spot.

In speaking about the surly answer I had received
from the man on the banks of the river, I said: "I
wonder why those men are camped there?   They must
have been there for several days."

Partner replied: "They are all out of grub and are
waiting for some one to come by to whack-up with 'em.
One of the fellows came out and talked with me and
said he had nothing left but beans, and tried to buy some
flour of me."

This opened up an entirely new line of thought.   I
understood now that what I had taken for sullenness
was the dejection of despair.   The way was growing
gloomy and dark to them.   They, too, were racing with
the wolf.

We had one short moment of relief next day as we
entered a lovely little meadow and camped for noon.
The sun shone warm, the grass was thick and sweet.
It was like late April in the central West — cool,

fragrant, silent. Aisles of peaks stretched behind us and before us. We were still high in the mountains, and the country was less wooded and more open. But we left this beautiful spot and entered again on a morass. It was a day of torture to man and beast. The land continued silent. There were no toads, no butterflies, no insects of any kind, except a few mosquitoes, no crickets, no singing thing. I have never seen a land so empty of life. We had left even the whistling marmots entirely behind us.

We travelled now four outfits together, with some twenty-five horses. Part of the time I led with Ladrone, part of the time "The Man from Chihuahua" took the lead, with his fine strong bays. If a horse got down we all swarmed around and lifted him out, and when any question of the trail came up we held "conferences of the powers."

We continued for the most part up a wide mossy and grassy river bottom covered with water. We waded for miles in water to our ankles, crossing hundreds of deep little rivulets. Occasionally a horse went down into a hole and had to be "snailed out," and we were wet and covered with mud all day. It was a new sort of trail and a terror. The mountains on each side were very stately and impressive, but we could pay little attention to views when our horses were miring down at every step.

We could not agree about the river. Some were inclined to the belief that it was a branch of the Stikeen, the old man was sure it was "Skeeny." We were troubled by a new sort of fly, a little orange-colored fellow whose habits were similar to those of the little black fiends of the Bulkley Valley. They were very poisonous indeed, and made our ears swell up enormously — the itching and burning was well-nigh intolerable. We saw no life at all save one grouse hen guarding her young. A paradise for game it seemed, but no game. A beautiful grassy, marshy, and empty land. We passed over one low divide after another with immense snowy peaks thickening all around us. For the first time in over two hundred miles we were all able to ride. Whistling marmots and grouse again abounded. We had a bird at every meal. The wind was cool and the sky was magnificent, and for the first time in many days we were able to take off our hats and face the wind in exultation.

Toward night, however, mosquitoes became troublesome in their assaults, covering the horses in solid masses. Strange to say, none of them, not even Ladrone, seemed to mind them in the least. We felt sure now of having left the Skeena forever. One day we passed over a beautiful little spot of dry ground, which filled us with delight; it seemed as though we had reached the prairies of the pamphlets. We camped there for noon, and though the mosquitoes were terrific we were all chortling with joy. The horses found grass in plenty and plucked up spirits amazingly. We were deceived. In half an hour we were in the mud again.

The whole country for miles and miles in every direction was a series of high open valleys almost entirely above timber line. These valleys formed the starting-points of innumerable small streams which fell away into the Iskoot on the left, the Stikeen on the north, the Skeena on the east and south. These valleys were covered with grass and moss intermingled, and vast tracts were flooded with water from four to eight inches deep, through which we were forced to slop hour after hour, and riding was practically impossible.

As we were plodding along silently one day a dainty white gull came lilting through the air and was greeted with cries of joy by the weary drivers. More than one of them could " smell the salt water." In imagination they saw this bird following the steamer up the Stikeen to the first south fork, thence to meet us. It seemed only a short ride down the valley to the city of Glenora and the post-office.

Each day we drove above timber line, and at noon were forced to rustle the dead dwarf pine for fire. The marshes were green and filled with exquisite flowers and mosses, little white and purple bells, some of them the most beautiful turquoise-green rising from tufts of verdure like mignonette. I observed also a sort of crocus and some cheery little buttercups. The ride would have been magnificent had it not been for the spongy, sloppy marsh through which our horses toiled. As it was, we felt a certain breadth and grandeur in it surpassing anything we had hitherto seen. Our three outfits with some score of horses went winding through the wide, green, treeless valleys with tinkle of bells and sharp cry of drivers. The trail was difficult to follow, because in the open ground each man before us had to take his own course, and there were few signs to mark the line the road-gang had taken.

It was impossible to tell where we were, but I was certain we were upon the head-waters of some one of the many forks of the great Stikeen River. Marmots and a sort of little prairie dog continued plentiful, but there was no other life. The days were bright and cool, resplendent with sun and rich in grass.

Some of the goldseekers fired a salute with shotted guns when; poised on the mountain side, they looked down upon a stream flowing to the northwest. But the joy was short-lived. The descent of this mountain's side was by all odds the most terrible piece of trail we had yet found. It led down the north slope, and was oozy and slippery with the melting snow. It dropped in short zigzags down through a grove of tangled, gnarled, and savage cedars and pines, whose roots were like iron and filled with spurs that were sharp as chisels. The horses, sliding upon their haunches and unable to turn themselves in the mud, crashed into the tangled pines and were in danger of being torn to pieces. For more than an hour we slid and slewed through this horrible jungle of savage trees, and when we came out below we had two horses badly snagged in the feet, but Ladrone was uninjured.

We now crossed and recrossed the little stream, which dropped into a deep cañon running still to the northwest. After descending for some hours we took a trail which branched sharply to the northeast, and climbed heavily to a most beautiful camping-spot between the peaks, with good grass, and water, and wood all around us.

We were still uncertain of our whereabouts, but all the boys were fairly jubilant. "This would be a splendid camp for a few weeks," said partner.

That night as the sun set in incommunicable splendor over the snowy peaks to the west the empty land seemed left behind. We went to sleep with the sound of a near-by mountain stream in our ears, and the voice of an eagle sounding somewhere on the high cliffs.

The next day we crossed another divide and entered another valley running north. Being confident that this *was* the Stikeen, we camped early and put our little house up. It was raining a little. We had descended again to the aspens and clumps of wild roses. It was good to see their lovely faces once more after our long stay in the wild, cold valleys of the upper lands. The whole country seemed drier, and the vegetation quite different. Indeed, it resembled some of the Colorado valleys, but was less barren on the bottoms. There were still no insects, no crickets, no bugs, and very few birds of any kind.

All along the way on the white surface of the blazed trees were messages left by those who had gone before us. Some of them were profane assaults upon the road-gang. Others were pathetic inquiries: "Where in hell are we?" — "How is this for a prairie route?" — "What river is this, anyhow?" To these pencillings others had added facetious replies. There were also warnings and signs to help us keep out of the mud.

We followed the same stream all day. Whether the Iskoot or not we did not know. The signs of lower altitude thickened. Wild roses met us again, and strawberry blossoms starred the sunny slopes. The grass was dry and ripe, and the horses did not relish it after their long stay in the juicy meadows above. We had been wet every day for nearly three weeks, and did not mind moisture now, but my shoes were rapidly going to pieces, and my last pair of trousers was frazzled to the knees.

Nearly every outfit had lame horses like our old bay, hobbling along bravely. Our grub was getting very light, which was a good thing for the horses; but we had an occasional grouse to fry, and so as long as our flour held out we were well fed.

It became warmer each day, and some little weazened berries appeared on the hillsides, the first we had seen, and they tasted mighty good after months of bacon and beans. We were taking some pleasure in the trip again, and had it not been for the sores on our horses' feet and our scant larder we should have been quite at ease. Our course now lay parallel to a range of peaks on our right, which we figured to be the Hotailub Mountains. This settled the question of our position on the map — we were on the third and not the first south fork of the Stikeen and were a long way still from Telegraph Creek.

We tunnelled miles of silent pines,
　Dark forests where the stillness was so deep
The scared wind walked a tip-toe on the spines,
　And the restless aspen seemed to sleep.

We threaded aisles of dripping fir;
　We climbed toward mountains dim and far,
Where snow forever shines and shines,
　And only winds and waters are.

Red streams came down from hillsides crissed and crossed
　With fallen firs; but on a sudden, lo!
A silver lakelet bound and barred
　With sunset's clouds reflected far below.

These lakes so lonely were, so still and cool,
　They burned as bright as burnished steel;
The shadowed pine branch in the pool
　Was no less vivid than the real.

We crossed the great divide and saw
　The sun-lit valleys far below us wind;
Before us opened cloudless sky; the raw,
　Gray rain swept close behind.

We saw great glaciers grind themselves to foam;
　We trod the moose's lofty home,
And heard, high on the yellow hills,
　The wildcat clamor of his ills.

The way grew grimmer day by day,
　The weeks to months stretched on and on;
And hunger kept, not far away,
　A never failing watch at dawn.

We lost all reckoning of season and of time;
　Sometimes it seemed the bitter breeze
Of icy March brought fog and rain,
　And next November tempests shook the trees.

It was a wild and lonely ride.
　Save the hid loon's mocking cry,
Or marmot on the mountain side,
　The earth was silent as the sky.

All day through sunless forest aisles,
　On cold dark moss our horses trod;
It was so lonely there for miles and miles,
　The land seemed lost to God.

Our horses cut by rocks; by brambles torn,
　Staggered onward, stiff and sore;
Or broken, bruised, and saddle-worn,
　Fell in the sloughs to rise no more.

Yet still we rode right on and on,
　And shook our clenched hands at the clouds,
Daring the winds of early dawn,
　And the dread torrent roaring loud.

So long we rode, so hard, so far,
  We seemed condemned by stern decree
To ride until the morning star
  Should sink forever in the sea.

Yet now, when all is past, I dream
  Of every mountain's shining cap.
I long to hear again the stream
  Roar through the foam-white granite gap.

The pains recede.   The joys draw near.
  The splendors of great Nature's face
Make me forget all need, all fear,
  And the long journey grows in grace.

THE GREETING OF THE ROSES

We had been long in mountain snow,
In valleys bleak, and broad, and bare,
Where only moss and willows grow,
And no bird wings the silent air.
And so when on our downward way,
Wild roses met us, we were glad;
They were so girlish fair, so gay,
It seemed the sun had made them mad.

CHAPTER XVII

THE WOLVES AND THE VULTURES ASSEMBLE

ABOUT noon of the fiftieth day out, we came down to the bank of a tremendously swift stream which we called the third south fork. On a broken paddle stuck in the sand we found this notice: "The trail crosses here. Swim horses from the bar. It is supposed to be about ninety miles to Telegraph Creek.—(Signed) The Mules."

We were bitterly disappointed to find ourselves so far from our destination, and began once more to calculate on the length of time it would take us to get out of the wilderness.

Partner showed me the flour-sack which he held in one brawny fist. "I believe the dern thing leaks," said he, and together we went over our store of food. We found ourselves with an extra supply of sugar, condensed cream, and other things which our friends the Manchester boys needed, while they were able to spare us a little flour. There was a tacit agreement that we should travel together and stand together. Accordingly we began to plan for the crossing of this swift and dangerous stream. A couple of canoes were found cached in the bushes, and these would enable us to set our goods across, while we forced our horses to swim from a big bar in the stream above.

While we were discussing these thing around our fires at night, another tramper, thin and weak, came into camp. He was a little man with a curly red beard, and was exceedingly chipper and jocular for one in his condition. He had been out of food for some days, and had been living on squirrels, ground-hogs, and such other small deer as he could kill and roast along his way. He brought word of considerable suffering among the outfits behind us, reporting " The Dutchman " to be entirely out of beans and flour, while others had lost so many of their horses that all were in danger of starving to death in the mountains.

As he warmed up on coffee and beans, he became very amusing.

He was hairy and ragged, but neat, and his face showed a certain delicacy of physique. He, too, was a marked example of the craze to " get somewhere where gold is." He broke off suddenly in the midst of his story to exclaim with great energy : " I want to do two things, go back and get my boy away from my wife, and break the back of my brother-in-law. He made all the trouble."

Once and again he said, " I'm going to find the gold up here or lay my bones on the hills."

In the midst of these intense phrases he whistled gayly or broke off to attend to his cooking. He told of his hard experiences, with pride and joy, and said, " Isn't it lucky I caught you just here ? " and seemed willing to talk all night.

In the morning I went over to the campfire to see if he were still with us.   He was sitting in his scanty bed before the fire, mending his trousers.   " I've just got to put a patch on right now or my knee'll be through," he explained.   He had a neat little kit of materials and everything was in order.   " I haven't time to turn the edges of the patch under," he went on.   " It ought to be done — you can't make a durable patch unless you do.   This ' housewife ' my wife made me when we was first married.   I was peddlin' then in eastern Oregon. If it hadn't been for her brother — oh, I'll smash his face in, some day " — he held up the other trouser leg : " See that patch ?   Ain't that a daisy ? — that's the way I ought to do.   Say, looks like I ought to rustle enough grub out of all these outfits to last me into Glenora, don't it ? "

We came down gracefully — we could not withstand such prattle.   The blacksmith turned in some beans, the boys from Manchester divided their scanty store of flour and bacon, I brought some salt, some sugar, and some oatmeal, and as the small man put it away he chirped and chuckled like a cricket.   His thanks were mere words, his voice was calm.   He accepted our aid as a matter of course.   No perfectly reasonable man would ever take such frightful chances as this absurd little ass set his face to without fear.   He hummed a little tune as he packed his outfit into his shoulder-straps. " I ought to rattle into Glenora on this grub, hadn't I ? " he said.

At last he was ready to be ferried across the river,

which was swift and dangerous. Burton set him across, and as he was about to depart I gave him a letter to post and a half-dollar to pay postage. My name was written on the corner of the envelope. He knew me then and said, " I've a good mind to stay right with you; I'm something of a writer myself."

I hastened to say that he could reach Glenora two or three days in advance of us, for the reason that we were bothered with a lame horse. In reality, we were getting very short of provisions and were even then on rations. " I think you'll overtake the Borland outfit," I said. " If you don't, and you need help, camp by the road till we come up and we'll all share as long as there's anything to share. But you are in good trim and have as much grub as we have, so you'd better spin along."

He " hit the trail " with a hearty joy that promised well, and I never saw him again. His cheery smile and unshrinking cheek carried him through a journey that appalled old packers with tents, plenty of grub, and good horses. To me he was simply a strongly accentuated type of the goldseeker — insanely persistent ; blind to all danger, deaf to all warning, and doomed to failure at the start.

The next day opened cold and foggy, but we entered upon a hard day's work. Burton became the chief canoeman, while one of the Manchester boys, stripped to the undershirt, sat in the bow to pull at the paddle " all same Siwash." Burton's skill and good judgment enabled us to cross without losing so much as a buckle. Some of our poor lame horses had a hard struggle in the icy current.   At about 4 P.M. we were able to line up in the trail on the opposite side.   We pressed on up to the higher valleys in hopes of finding better feed, and camped in the rain about two miles from the ford.   The wind came from the northwest with a suggestion of autumn in its uneasy movement.   The boys were now exceedingly anxious to get into the gold country.   They began to feel most acutely the passing of the summer. In the camp at night the talk was upon the condition of Telegraph Creek and the Teslin Lake Trail.

Rain, rain, rain !   It seemed as though no day could pass without rain.   And as I woke I heard the patter of fine drops on our tent roof.   The old man cursed the weather most eloquently, expressing the general feeling of the whole company.   However, we saddled up and pushed on, much delayed by the lame horses.

At about twelve o'clock I missed my partner's voice and looking about saw only two of the packhorses following.   Hitching those beside the trail, I returned to find Burton seated beside the lame horse, which could not cross the slough.   I examined the horse's foot and found a thin stream of arterial blood spouting out.

" That ends it, Burton," I said.   " I had hoped to bring all my horses through, but this old fellow is out of the race.   It is a question now either of leaving him beside the trail with a notice to have him brought forward or of shooting him out of hand."

To this partner gravely agreed, but said, " It's going to be pretty hard lines to shoot that faithful old chap."

" Yes," I replied, " I confess I haven't the courage

to face him with a rifle after all these weeks of faithful service. But it must be done. You remember that horse back there with a hole in his flank and his head flung up? We mustn't leave this old fellow to be a prey to the wolves. Now if you'll kill him you can set your price on the service. Anything at all I will pay. Did you ever kill a horse?"

Partner was honest. "Yes, once. He was old and sick and I believed it better to put him out of his suffering than to let him drag on."

"That settles it, partner," said I. "Your hands are already imbued with gore — it must be done."

He rose with a sigh. "All right. Lead him out into the thicket."

I handed him the gun (into which I had shoved two steel-jacketed bullets, the kind that will kill a grizzly bear), and took the old horse by the halter. "Come, boy," I said, "it's hard, but it's the only merciful thing." The old horse looked at me with such serene trust and confidence, my courage almost failed me. His big brown eyes were so full of sorrow and patient endurance. With some urging he followed me into the thicket a little aside from the trail. Turning away I mounted Ladrone in order that I might not see what happened. There was a crack of a rifle in the bush — the sound of a heavy body falling, and a moment later Burton returned with a coiled rope in his hand and a look of trouble on his face. The horses lined up again with one empty place and an extra saddle topping the pony's pack. It was a sorrowful thing to do, but there

was no better way.   As I rode on, looking back occasionally to see that my train was following, my heart
ached to think of the toil the poor old horse had under-
gone — only to meet death in the bush at the hands
of his master.

Relieved of our wounded horse we made good time
and repassed before nine o'clock several outfits that had
overhauled us during our trouble.   We rose higher and
higher, and came at last into a grassy country and to a
series of small lakes, which were undoubtedly the source
of the second fork of the Stikeen.   But as we had lost
so much time during the day, we pushed on with all our
vigor for a couple of hours and camped about nine
o'clock of a beautiful evening, with a magnificent sky
arching us as if with a prophecy of better times ahead.

The horses were now travelling very light, and our
food supply was reduced to a few pounds of flour and
bread — we had no game and no berries.   Beans were
all gone and our bacon reduced to the last shred.   We
had come to expect rain every day of our lives, and were
feeling a little the effects of our scanty diet of bread and
bacon — hill-climbing was coming to be laborious.   However, the way led downward most of the time, and we
were able to rack along at a very good pace even on an
empty stomach.

During the latter part of the second day the trail led
along a high ridge, a sort of hog-back overlooking a
small river valley on our left, and bringing into view an
immense blue cañon far ahead of us.   "There lies the
Stikeen," I called to Burton.   "We're on the second

south fork, which we follow to the Stikeen, thence to the left to Telegraph Creek." I began to compose doggerel verses to express our exultation.

We were very tired and glad when we reached a camping-place. We could not stop on this high ridge for lack of water, although the feed was very good. We were forced to plod on and on until we at last descended into the valley of a little stream which crossed our path. The ground had been much trampled, but as rain was falling and darkness coming on, there was nothing to do but camp.

Out of our last bit of bacon grease and bread and tea we made our supper. While we were camping, " The Wild Dutchman," a stalwart young fellow we had seen once or twice on the trail, came by with a very sour visage. He went into camp near, and came over to see us. He said: " I hain't had no pread for more dan a veek. I've nuttin' put peans. If you can, let me haf a biscuit. By Gott, how goot dat vould taste."

I yielded up a small loaf and encouraged him as best I could: " As I figure it, we are within thirty-five miles of Telegraph Creek; I've kept a careful diary of our travel. If we've passed over the Dease Lake Trail, which is probably about four hundred miles from Hazleton to Glenora, we must be now within thirty-five miles of Telegraph Creek."

I was not half so sure of this as I made him think; but it gave him a great deal of comfort, and he went off very much enlivened.

Sunday and no sun! It was raining when we awoke

and the mosquitoes were stickier than ever.   Our grub was nearly gone, our horses thin and weak, and the journey uncertain.   All ill things seemed to assemble like vultures to do us harm.   The world was a grim place that day.   It was a question whether we were not still on the third south fork instead of the second south fork, in which case we were at least one hundred miles from our supplies.   If we were forced to cross the main Stikeen and go down on the other side, it might be even farther.

The men behind us were all suffering, and some of them were sure to have a hard time if such weather continued.   At the same time I felt comparatively sure of our ground.

We were ragged, dirty, lame, unshaven, and unshorn — we were fighting from morning till night.   The trail became more discouraging each moment that the rain continued to fall.   There was little conversation even between partner and myself.   For many days we had moved in perfect silence for the most part, though no gloom or sullenness appeared in Burton's face.   We were now lined up once more, taking the trail without a word save the sharp outcry of the drivers hurrying the horses forward, or the tinkle of the bells on the lead horse of the train.

THE VULTURE

He wings a slow and watchful flight,
His neck is bare, his eyes are bright,
His plumage fits the starless night.

He sits at feast where cattle lie
Withering in ashen alkali,
And gorges till he scarce can fly.

But he is kingly on the breeze!
On rigid wing, in careless ease,
A soundless bark on viewless seas.
Piercing the purple storm cloud, he makes
The sun his neighbor, and shakes
His wrinkled neck in mock dismay,
And swings his slow, contemptuous way
Above the hot red lightning's play.

Monarch of cloudland — yet a ghoul of prey.

CAMPFIRES

1. *Popple*

A river curves like a bended bow,
And over it winds of summer lightly blow;
Two boys are feeding a flame with bark
Of the pungent popple.   Hark!
They are uttering dreams.   " I
Will go hunt gold toward the western sky,'
Says the older lad; "I know it is there,
For the rainbow shows just where
It is.   I'll go camping, and take a pan,
And shovel gold, when I'm a man."

2. *Sage Brush*

The burning day draws near its end,
And on the plain a man and his friend
Sit feeding an odorous sage-brush fire.
A lofty butte like a funeral pyre,
With the sun atop, looms high
In the cloudless, windless, saffron sky.
A snake sleeps under a grease-wood plant;
A horned toad snaps at a passing ant;
The plain is void as a polar floe,
And the limitless sky has a furnace glow.

The men are gaunt and shaggy and gray,
And their childhood river is far away;
The gold still hides at the rainbow's tip,
Yet the wanderer speaks with a resolute lip.
" I will seek till I find — or till I die,"
He mutters, and lifts his clenched hand high,
And puts behind him love and wife,
And the quiet round of a farmer's life.

3. *Pine*

The dark day ends in a bitter night.
The mighty mountains cold, and white,
And stern as avarice, still hide their gold
Deep in wild cañons fold on fold,
Both men are old, and one is grown
As gray as the snows around him sown.
He hovers over a fire of pine,
Spicy and cheering; toward the line
Of the towering peaks he lifts his eyes.
" I'd rather have a boy with shining hair,
To bear my name, than all your share
Of earth's red gold," he said;
And died, a loveless, childless man,
Before the morning light began.

CHAPTER XVIII

AT LAST THE STIKEEN

ABOUT the middle of the afternoon of the fifty-eighth day we topped a low divide, and came in sight of the Stikeen River. Our hearts thrilled with pleasure as we looked far over the deep blue and purple-green spread of valley, dim with mist, in which a little silver ribbon of water could be seen.

After weeks of rain, as if to make amend for useless severity, the sun came out, a fresh westerly breeze sprang up, and the sky filled with glowing clouds flooded with tender light. The bloom of fireweed almost concealed the devastation of flame in the fallen firs, and the grim forest seemed a royal road over which we could pass as over a carpet — winter seemed far away.

But all this was delusion. Beneath us lay a thousand quagmires. The forest was filled with impenetrable jungles and hidden streams, ridges sullen and silent were to be crossed, and the snow was close at hand. Across this valley an eagle might sweep with joy, but the pack trains must crawl in mud and mire through long hours of torture. We spent but a moment here, and then with grim resolution called out, " Line up, boys, line up!" and struck down upon the last two days of our long journey.

On the following noon we topped another rise, and came unmistakably in sight of the Stikeen River lying deep in its rocky cañon. We had ridden all the morning in a pelting rain, slashed by wet trees, plunging through bogs and sliding down ravines, and when we saw the valley just before us we raised a cheer. It seemed we could hear the hotel bells ringing far below.

But when we had tumbled down into the big cañon near the water's edge, we found ourselves in scarcely better condition than before. We were trapped with no feed for our horses, and no way to cross the river, which was roaring mad by reason of the heavy rains, a swift and terrible flood, impossible to swim. Men were camped all along the bank, out of food like ourselves, and ragged and worn and weary. They had formed a little street of camps. Borland, the leader of the big mule train, was there, calm and efficient as ever. "The Wilson Outfit," "The Man from Chihuahua," "Throw-me-feet," and the Manchester boys were also included in the group. "The Dutchman" came sliding down just behind us.

After a scanty dinner of bacon grease and bread we turned our horses out on the flat by the river, and joined the little village. Borland said: "We've been here for a day and a half, tryin' to induce that damn ferryman to come over, and now we're waitin' for reënforcements. Let's try it again, numbers will bring 'em."

Thereupon we marched out solemnly upon the bank

(some ten or fifteen of us) and howled like a pack of wolves.

For two hours we clamored, alternating the Ute war-whoop with the Swiss yodel. It was truly cacophonous, but it produced results. Minute figures came to the brow of the hill opposite, and looked at us like cautious cockroaches and then went away. At last two shadowy beetles crawled down the zigzag trail to the ferry-boat, and began bailing her out. Ultimately three men, sweating, scared, and tremulous, swung a clumsy scow upon the sand at our feet. It was no child's play to cross that stream. Together with one of "The Little Dutchmen," and a representation from "The Mule Outfit," I stepped into the boat and it was swung off into the savage swirl of gray water. We failed of landing the first time. I did not wonder at the ferryman's nervousness, as I felt the heave and rush of the whirling savage flood.

At the "ratty" little town of Telegraph Creek we purchased beans at fifteen cents a pound, bacon at thirty-five cents, and flour at ten cents, and laden with these necessaries hurried back to the hungry hordes on the opposite side of the river. That night "The Little Dutchman" did nothing but cook and eat to make up for lost time. Every face wore a smile.

The next morning Burton and one or two other men from the outfits took the horses back up the trail to find feed, while the rest of us remained in camp to be ready for the boats. Late in the afternoon we heard far down the river a steamer whistling for Telegraph

N

Creek, and everybody began packing truck down to the river where the boat was expected to land. Word was sent back over the trail to the boys herding the horses, and every man was in a tremor of apprehension lest the herders should not hear the boat and bring the horses down in time to get off on it.

It was punishing work packing our stuff down the sloppy path to the river bank, but we buckled to it hard, and in the course of a couple of hours had all snug and ready for embarkation.

There was great excitement among the outfits, and every man was hurrying and worrying to get away. It was known that charges would be high, and each of us felt in his pocket to see how many dollars he had left. The steamboat company had us between fire and water and could charge whatever it pleased. Some of the poor prospectors gave up their last dollar to cross this river toward which they had journeyed so long.

The boys came sliding down the trail wildly excited, driving the horses before them, and by 5.30 we were all packed on the boat, one hundred and twenty horses and some two dozen men. We were a seedy and careworn lot, in vivid contrast with the smartly uniformed purser of the boat. The rates were exorbitant, but there was nothing to do but to pay them. However, Borland and I, acting as committee, brought such pressure to bear upon the purser that he "threw in" a dinner, and there was a joyous rush for the table when this good news was announced. For the first time in nearly three months we were able to sit down to a fairly good meal with clean nice tableware, with pie and pudding to end the meal. It seemed as though we had reached civilization. The boat was handsomely built, and quite new and capacious, too, for it held our horses without serious crowding. I was especially anxious about Ladrone, but was able to get him into a very nice place away from the engines and in no danger of being kicked by a vicious mule.

We drifted down the river past Telegraph Creek without stopping, and late at night laid by at Glenora and unloaded in the crisp, cool dusk. As we came off the boat with our horses we were met by a crowd of cynical loafers who called to us out of the dark, " What in hell you fellows think you're doing? " We were regarded as wildly insane for having come over so long and tedious a route.

We erected our tents, and went into camp beside our horses on the bank near the dock. It was too late to move farther that night. We fed our beasts upon hay at five cents a pound, — poor hay at that, — and they were forced to stand exposed to the searching river wind.

As for ourselves, we were filled with dismay by the hopeless dulness of the town. Instead of being the hustling, rushing gold camp we had expected to find, it came to light as a little town of tents and shanties, filled with men who had practically given up the Teslin Lake Route as a bad job. The government trail was incomplete, the wagon road only built halfway, and the railroad — of which we had heard so much talk — had been abandoned altogether.

As I slipped the saddle and bridle from Ladrone next day and turned him out upon the river bottom for a two weeks' rest, my heart was very light. The long trail was over. No more mud, rocks, stumps, and roots for Ladrone. Away the other poor animals streamed down the trail, many of them lame, all of them poor and weak, and some of them still crazed by the poisonous plants of the cold green mountains through which they had passed.

This ended the worst of the toil, the torment of the trail. It had no dangers, but it abounded in worriments and disappointments. As I look back upon it now I suffer, because I see my horses standing ankle-deep in water on barren marshes or crowding round the fire chilled and weak, in endless rain. If our faces looked haggard and worn, it was because of the never ending anxiety concerning the faithful animals who trusted in us to find them food and shelter. Otherwise we suffered little, slept perfectly dry and warm every night, and ate three meals each day : true, the meals grew scanty and monotonous, but we did not go hungry.

The trail was a disappointment to me, not because it was long and crossed mountains, but because it ran through a barren, monotonous, silent, gloomy, and rainy country. It ceased to interest me. It had almost no wild animal life, which I love to hear and see. Its lakes and rivers were for the most part cold and sullen, and its forests sombre and depressing. The only pleasant places after leaving Hazleton were the high valleys above timber line. They were magnificent, although wet and marshy to traverse.

As a route to reach the gold fields of Teslin Lake and the Yukon it is absurd and foolish. It will never be used again for that purpose. Should mines develop on the high divides between the Skeena, Iskoot, and Stikeen, it may possibly be used again from Hazleton; otherwise it will be given back to the Indians and their dogs.

A man put love forth from his heart,
　　And rode across the desert far away.
"Woman shall have no place nor part
　　In my lone life," men heard him say.
He rode right on. The level rim
　　Of the barren plain grew low and wide;
It seemed to taunt and beckon him,
　　To ride right on and fiercely ride.

One day he rode a well-worn path,
　　And lo! even in that far land
He saw (and cursed in gusty wrath)
　　A woman's footprint in the sand.
Sharply he drew the swinging rein,
　　And hanging from his saddle bow
Gazed long and silently — cursed again,
　　Then turned as if to go.

"For love will seize you at the end,
　　Fear loneliness — fear sickness, too,
For they will teach you wisdom, friend."
　　Yet he rode on as madmen do.
He built a cabin by a sounding stream,
　　He digged in cañons dark and deep,
And ever the waters caused a dream
　　And the face of woman broke his sleep.

It was a slender little mark,
   And the man had lived alone so long
Within the cañon's noise and dark,
   The footprint moved him like a song.
It spoke to him of women in the East,
   Of girls in silken robes, with shining hair,
And talked of those who sat at feast,
   While sweet-eyed laughter filled the air.

And more.   A hundred visions rose,
   He saw his mother's knotted hands
Ply round thick-knitted homely hose,
   Her thoughts with him in desert lands.
A smiling wife, in bib and cap,
   Moved busily from chair to chair,
Or sat with apples in her lap,
   Content with sweet domestic care.

All these his curse had put away,
   All these were his no more to hold ;
He had his cañon cold and gray,
   He had his little heaps of gold.

CHAPTER XIX

THE GOLDSEEKERS' CAMP AT GLENORA

GLENORA, like Telegraph Creek, was a village of tents and shacks. Previous to the opening of the year it had been an old Hudson Bay trading-post at the head of navigation on the Stikeen River, but during April and May it had been turned into a swarming camp of goldseekers on their way to Teslin Lake by way of the much-advertised "Stikeen Route" to the Yukon.

A couple of months before our arrival nearly five thousand people had been encamped on the river flat; but one disappointment had followed another, the government road had been abandoned, the pack trail had proved a menace, and as a result the camp had thinned away, and when we of the Long Trail began to drop into town Glenora contained less than five hundred people, including tradesmen and mechanics.

The journey of those who accompanied me on the Long Trail was by no means ended. It was indeed only half done. There remained more than one hundred and seventy miles of pack trail before the head of navigation on the Yukon could be reached. I turned aside. My partner went on.

In order to enter the head-waters of the Pelly it was necessary to traverse four hundred miles of trail, over which a year's provision for each man must be carried. Food was reported to be " a dollar a pound " at Teslin Lake and winter was coming on. To set face toward any of these regions meant the most careful preparation or certain death.

The weather was cold and bleak, and each night the boys assembled around the big campfire to discuss the situation. They reported the country full of people eager to get away. Everybody seemed studying the problem of what to do and how to do it. Some were for going to the head-waters of the Pelly, others advocated the Nisutlin, and others still thought it a good plan to prospect on the head-waters of the Tooya, from which excellent reports were coming in.

Hour after hour they debated, argued, and agreed. In the midst of it all Burton remained cool and unhurried. Sitting in our tent, which flapped and quivered in the sounding southern wind, we discussed the question of future action. I determined to leave him here with four of the horses and a thousand pounds of grub with which to enter the gold country; for my partner was a miner, not a literary man.

It had been my intention to go with him to Teslin Lake, there to build a boat and float down the river to Dawson; but I was six weeks behind my schedule, the trail was reported to be bad, and the water in the Hotalinqua very low, making boating slow and hazardous. Therefore I concluded to join the stream of goldseekers who were pushing down toward the coast to go in by way of Skagway.

There was a feeling in the air on the third day after going into camp which suggested the coming of autumn. Some of the boys began to dread the desolate north, out of which the snows would soon begin to sweep. It took courage to set face into that wild land with winter coming on, and yet many of them were ready to do it. The Manchester boys and Burton formed a " side-part-nership," and faced a year of bacon and beans without visible sign of dismay.

The ominous cold deepened a little every night. It seemed like October as the sun went down. Around us on every side the mountain peaks cut the sky keen as the edge of a sword, and the wind howled up the river gusty and wild.

A little group of tents sprang up around our own and every day was full of quiet enjoyment. We were all living very high, with plenty of berries and an occasional piece of fresh beef. Steel-head salmon were running and were a drug in the market.

The talk of the Pelly River grew excited as a report came in detailing a strike, and all sorts of outfits began to sift out along the trail toward Teslin Lake. The rain ceased at last and the days grew very pleasant with the wind again in the south, roaring up the river all day long with great power, reminding me of the equatorial currents which sweep over Illinois and Wisconsin in September. We had nothing now to trouble us but the question of moving out into the gold country.

One by one the other misguided ones of the Long Trail came dropping into camp to meet the general depression and stagnation. They were brown, ragged, long-haired, and for the most part silent with dismay. Some of them celebrated their escape by getting drunk, but mainly they were too serious-minded to waste time or substance. Some of them had expended their last dollar on the trail and were forced to sell their horses for money to take them out of the country. Some of the partnerships went to pieces for other causes. Long-smouldering dissensions burst into flame. "The Swedes" divided and so did "The Dutchman," the more resolute of them keeping on the main trail while others took the trail to the coast or returned to the States.

Meanwhile, Ladrone and his fellows were rejoicing like ourselves in fairly abundant food and in continuous rest. The old gray began to look a little more like his own proud self. As I went out to see him he came up to me to be curried and nosed about me, begging for salt. His trust in me made him doubly dear, and I took great joy in thinking that he, at least, was not doomed to freeze or starve in this savage country which has no mercy and no hope for horses.

There was great excitement on the first Sunday following our going into camp, when the whistle of a steamer announced the coming of the mail. It produced as much movement as an election or a bear fight. We all ran to the bank to see her struggle with the current, gaining headway only inch by inch. She was a small stern-wheeler, not unlike the boats which run on the upper Missouri.   We all followed her down to the Hudson Bay post, like a lot of small boys at a circus, to see her unload.   This was excitement enough for one day, and we returned to camp feeling that we were once more in touch with civilization.

Among the first of those who met us on our arrival was a German, who was watching some horses and some supplies in a big tent close by the river bank.   While pitching my tent on that first day he came over to see me, and after a few words of greeting said quietly, but with feeling, " I am glad you've come, it was so lonesome here."   We were very busy, but I think we were reasonably kind to him in the days that followed. He often came over of an evening and stood about the fire, and although I did not seek to entertain him, I am glad to say I answered him civilly; Burton was even social.

I recall these things with a certain degree of feeling, because not less than a week later this poor fellow was discovered by one of our company swinging from the crosstree of the tent, a ghastly corpse.   There was something inexplicable in the deed.   No one could account for it.   He seemed not to be a man of deep feeling.   And one of the last things he uttered in my hearing was a coarse jest which I did not like and to which I made no reply.

In his pocket the coroner found a letter wherein he had written, " Bury me right here where I failed, here on the bank of the river."   It contained also a message to his wife and children in the States.   There were tragic splashes of red on the trail, murder, and violent death by animals and by swift waters. Now here at the end of the trail was a suicide.

> So this is the end of the trail to him —
> To swing at the tail of a rope and die ;
> Making a chapter gray and grim,
> Adding a ghost to the midnight sky ?
> He toiled for days on the icy way,
> He slept at night on the wind-swept snow;
> Now here he hangs in the morning's gray,
> A grisly shape by the river's flow.

It was just two weeks later when I put the bridle and saddle on Ladrone and rode him down the trail. His heart was light as mine, and he had gained some part of his firm, proud, leaping walk. He had confidence in the earth once more. This was the first firm stretch of road he had trod for many weeks. He was now to take the boat for the outside world.

There was an element of sadness in the parting between Ladrone and the train he had led for so many miles. As we saddled up for the last time he stood waiting. The horses had fared together for ninety days. They had "lined up" nearly two hundred times, and now for the last time I called out : " Line up, boys ! Line up ! Heke ! Heke ! "

Ladrone swung into the trail. Behind him came " Barney," next " Major," then sturdy " Bay Bill," and lastly " Nibbles," the pony. For the last time they were to follow their swift gray leader, who was going south to live at ease, while they must begin again the ascent of the trail.

Ladrone whinnied piteously for his mates as I led him aboard the steamer, but they did not answer. They were patiently waiting their master's signal. Never again would they set eyes on the stately gray leader who was bound to most adventurous things. Never again would they see the green grass come on the hills.

I had a feeling that I could go on living this way, leading a pack train across the country indefinitely. It seemed somehow as though this way of life, this routine, must continue. I had a deep interest in the four horses, and it was not without a feeling of guilt that I saw them move away on their last trail. At bottom the end of every horse is tragic. Death comes sooner or later, but death here in this country, so cold and bleak and pitiless to all animals, seems somehow closer, more inevitable, more cruel, and flings over every animal the shadow of immediate tragedy. There was something approaching crime in bringing a horse over that trail for a thousand miles only to turn him loose at the end, or to sell him to some man who would work him to the point of death, and then shoot him or turn him out to freeze.

As the time came when I must return to the south and to the tame, the settled, the quiet, I experienced a profound feeling of regret, of longing for the wild and lonely. I looked up at the shining green and white mountains and they allured me still, notwithstanding all the toil and discomfort of the journey just completed. The wind from the south, damp and cool, the great river gliding with rushing roar to meet the sea, had a distinct and wonderful charm from which I rent myself with distinct effort.

THE TOIL OF THE TRAIL

What have I gained by the toil of the trail?
I know and know well.
I have found once again the lore I had lost
In the loud city's hell.

I have broadened my hand to the cinch and the axe,
I have laid my flesh to the rain;
I was hunter and trailer and guide;
I have touched the most primitive wildness again.

I have threaded the wild with the stealth of the deer,
No eagle is freer than I;
No mountain can thwart me, no torrent appall,
I defy the stern sky.
So long as I live these joys will remain,
I have touched the most primitive wildness again.

CHAPTER XX

GREAT NEWS AT WRANGELL

BOAT after boat had come up, stopped for a night, and dropped down the river again, carrying from ten to twenty of the goldseekers who had determined to quit or to try some other way in; and at last the time had come for me to say good-by to Burton and all those who had determined to keep on to Teslin Lake. I had helped them buy and sack and weigh their supplies, and they were ready to line up once more.

As I led Ladrone down toward the boat, he called again for his fellows, but only strangers made reply. After stowing him safely away and giving him feed, I returned to the deck in order to wave my hat to Burton.

In accordance with his peculiar, undemonstrative temperament, he stood for a few moments in silence, with his hands folded behind his back, then, with a final wave of the hand, turned on his heel and returned to his work.

Farewells and advice more or less jocular rang across the rail of the boat between some ten or fifteen of us who had hit the new trail and those on shore.

" Good-by, boys; see you at Dawson."

"We'll beat you in yet," called Bill.   "Don't over-work."

"Let us know if you strike it!" shouted Frank.

"All right; you do the same," I replied.

As the boat swung out into the stream, and the little group on the bank faded swiftly away, I confess to a little dimness of the eyes.   I thought of the hardships toward which my uncomplaining partner was headed, and it seemed to me Nature was conspiring to crush him.

The trip down the river was exceedingly interesting. The stream grew narrower as we approached the coast range, and became at last very dangerous for a heavy boat such as the *Strathcona* was.   We were forced to lay by at last, some fifty miles down, on account of the terrific wind which roared in through the gap, making the steering of the big boat through the cañon very difficult.

At the point where we lay for the night a small creek came in.   Steel-headed salmon were running, and the creek was literally lined with bear tracks of great size, as far up as we penetrated.   These bears are said to be a sort of brown fishing bear of enormous bulk, as large as polar bears, and when the salmon are spawning in the upper waters of the coast rivers, they become so fat they can hardly move.   Certainly I have never been in a country where bear signs were so plentiful.   The wood was an almost impassable tangle of vines and undergrowth, and the thought of really finding a bear was appalling.

The Stikeen breaks directly through the coast range at right angles, like a battering-ram. Immense glaciers were on either side. One tremendous river of ice came down on our right, presenting a face wall apparently hundreds of feet in height and some miles in width. I should have enjoyed exploring this glacier, which is said to be one of the greatest on the coast.

The next day our captain, a bold and reckless man, carried us through to Wrangell by *walking* his boat over the sand bars on its paddle-wheel. I was exceedingly nervous, because if for any reason we had become stuck in mid river, it would have been impossible to feed La-drone or to take him ashore except by means of another steamer. However, all things worked together to bring us safely through, and in the afternoon of the second day we entered an utterly different world — the warm, wet coast country. The air was moist, the grasses and tall ferns were luxuriant, and the forest trees immense. Out into a sun-bright bay we swept with a feeling of being in safe waters once more, and rounded-to about sunset at a point on the island just above a frowzy little town. This was Wrangell Island and the town was Fort Wrangell, one of the oldest stations on the coast.

I had placed my horse under bond intending to send him through to Vancouver to be taken care of by the Hudson Bay Company. He was still a Canadian horse and so must remain upon the wharf over night. As he was very restless and uneasy, I camped down beside him on the planks.

I lay for a long time listening to the waters flowing under me and looking at the gray-blue sky, across which stars shot like distant rockets dying out in the deeps of the heavens in silence. An odious smell rose from the bay as the tide went out, a seal bawled in the distance, fishes flopped about in the pools beneath me, and a man playing a violin somewhere in the village added a melancholy note. I could hear the boys crying, "All about the war," and Ladrone continued restless and eager. Several times in the night, when he woke me with his trampling, I called to him, and hearing my voice he became quiet.

I took breakfast at a twenty-five cent "joint," where I washed out of a tin basin in an ill-smelling area. After breakfast I grappled with the customs man and secured the papers which made Ladrone an American horse, free to eat grass wherever it could be found under the stars and stripes. I started immediately to lead him to pasture, and this was an interesting and memorable experience.

There are no streets, that is to say no roads, in Wrangell. There are no carriages and no horses, not even donkeys. Therefore it was necessary for Ladrone to walk the perilous wooden sidewalks after me. This he did with all the dignity of a county judge, and at last we came upon grass, knee deep, rich and juicy.

Our passage through the street created a great sensation. Little children ran to the gates to look upon us. "There goes a horsie," they shouted. An old man stopped me on the street and asked me where I was taking "T'old 'orse." I told him I had already ridden him over a thousand miles and now he was travelling with me back to God's country. He looked at me in amazement, and walked off tapping his forehead as a sign that I must certainly "have wheels."

As I watched Ladrone at his feed an old Indian woman came along and smiled with amiable interest. At last she said, pointing to the other side of the village, "Over there muck-a-muck, hy-u muck-a-muck." She wished to see the horse eating the best grass there was to be had on the island.

A little later three or four native children came down the hill and were so amazed and so alarmed at the sight of this great beast feeding beside the walk that they burst into loud outcry and ran desperately away. They were not accustomed to horses. To them he was quite as savage in appearance as a polar bear.

In a short time everybody in the town knew of the old gray horse and his owner. I furnished a splendid topic for humorous conversation during the dull hours of the day.

Here again I came upon other gaunt and rusty-coated men from the Long Trail. They could be recognized at a glance by reason of their sombre faces and their undecided action. They could scarcely bring themselves to such ignominious return from a fruitless trip on which they had started with so much elation, and yet they hesitated about attempting any further adventure to the north, mainly because their horses had sold for so little and their expenses had been so great.

Many of them were nearly broken. In the days that followed they discussed the matter in subdued voices, sitting in the sun on the great wharf, sombrely looking out upon the bay.

On the third day a steamer came in from the north, buzzing with the news of another great strike not far from Skagway. Juneau, Dyea, as well as Skagway itself, were said to be almost deserted. Men were leaving the White Pass Railway in hundreds, and a number of the hands on the steamer herself had deserted under the excitement. Mingling with the passengers we eagerly extracted every drop of information possible. No one knew much about it, but they said all they knew and a good part of what they had heard, and when the boat swung round and disappeared in the moonlight, she left the goldseekers exultant and tremulous on the wharf.

They were now aflame with desire to take part in this new stampede, which seemed to be within their slender means, and I, being one of them and eager to see such a " stampede," took a final session with the customs collector, and prepared to board the next boat.

I arranged with Duncan McKinnon to have my old horse taken care of in his lot. I dug wells for him so that he should not lack for water, and treated him to a dish of salt, and just at sunset said good-by to him with another twinge of sadness and turned toward the wharf. He looked very lonely and sad standing there with drooping head in the midst of the stumps of his pasture lot. However, there was plenty of feed and half a dozen men volunteered to keep an eye on him.

"Don't worry, mon," said Donald McLane. "He'll be gettin' fat and strong on the juicy grass, whilst you're a-heavin' out the gold-dust."

There were about ten of us who lined up to the purser's window of the little steamer which came along that night and purchased second-class passage. The boat was very properly named the *Utopia*, and was so crowded with other goldseekers from down the coast, that we of the Long Trail were forced to put our beds on the floor of the little saloon in the stern of the boat which was called the "social room." We were all second-class, and we all lay down in rows on the carpet, covering every foot of space. Each man rolled up in his own blankets, and I was the object of considerable remark by reason of my mattress, which gave me as good a bed as the vessel afforded.

There was a great deal of noise on the boat, and its passengers, both men and women, were not of the highest type. There were several stowaways, and some of the women were not very nice as to their actions, and, rightly or wrongly, were treated with scant respect by the men, who were loud and vulgar for the most part. Sleep was difficult in the turmoil.

Though second-class passengers, strange to say, we came first at table and were very well fed. The boat ran entirely inside a long row of islands, and the water was smooth as a river. The mountains grew each moment more splendid as we neared Skagway, and the ride was most enjoyable. Whales and sharks interested us on the way. The women came to light next day, and on the whole were much better than I had inferred from the two or three who were the source of disturbance the night before. The men were not of much interest; they seemed petty and without character for the most part.

At Juneau we came into a still more mountainous country, and for the rest of the way the scenery was magnificent. Vast rivers of ice came curving down absolutely out of the clouds which hid the summits of the mountains — came curving in splendid lines down to the very water's edge. The sea was chill and gray, and as we entered the mouth of Lynn Canal a raw swift wind swept by, making us shiver with cold. The grim bronze-green mountains' sides formed a most impressive but forbidding scene.

It was nine o'clock the next morning as we swung to and unloaded ourselves upon one of the long wharves which run out from the town of Skagway toward the deep water. We found the town exceedingly quiet. Half the men had gone to the new strike. Stores were being tended by women, some small shops were closed entirely, and nearly every business firm had sent representatives into the new gold fields, which we now found to be on Atlin Lake.

It was difficult to believe that this wharf a few months before had been the scene of a bloody tragedy which involved the shooting of " Soapy Smith," the renowned robber and desperado. On the contrary, it seemed quite like any other town of its size in the States. The air was warm and delightful in midday, but toward night the piercing wind swept down from the high mountains, making an overcoat necessary.

A few men had returned from this new district, and were full of enthusiasm concerning the prospects. Their reports increased the almost universal desire to have a part in the stampede. The Iowa boys from the Long Trail wasted no time, but set about their own plans for getting in. They expected to reach the creek by sheer force and awkwardness.

They had determined to try the "cut-off," which left the wagon road and took off up the east fork of the Skagway River. Nearly three hundred people had already set out on this trail, and the boys felt sure of "making it all right — all right," though it led over a great glacier and into an unmapped region of swift streams. "After the Telegraph Trail," said Doc, "we're not easily scared."

It seemed to me a desperate chance, and I was not ready to enter upon such a trip with only such grub and clothing as could be carried upon my back; but it was the last throw of the dice for these young fellows. They had very little money left, and could not afford to hire pack trains; but by making a swift dash into the country, each hoped to get a claim. How they expected to hold it or use it after they got it, they were unable to say; but as they were out for gold, and here was a chance (even though it were but the slightest chance in the world) to secure a location, they accepted it with the sublime audacity of youth and ignorance. They saddled themselves with their packs, and with a cheery wave of the hand said "Good-by and good luck" and marched away in single file.

Just a week later I went round to see if any news of them had returned to their bunk house. I found their names on the register. They had failed. One of them set forth their condition of purse and mind by writing: "Dave Walters, Boone, Iowa. Busted and going home."

THE GOLDSEEKERS

I saw these dreamers of dreams go by,
I trod in their footsteps a space;
Each marched with his eyes on the sky,
Each passed with a light on his face.

They came from the hopeless and sad,
They faced the future and gold;
Some the tooth of want's wolf had made mad,
And some at the forge had grown old.

Behind them these serfs of the tool
The rags of their service had flung;
No longer of fortune the fool,
This word from each bearded lip rung:

"Once more I'm a man, I am free!
No man is my master, I say;
To-morrow I fail, it may be —
No matter, I'm freeman to-day."

They go to a toil that is sure,
To despair and hunger and cold;
Their sickness no warning can cure,
They are mad with a longing for gold.

The light will fade from each eye,
The smile from each face;
They will curse the impassible sky,
And the earth when the snow torrents race.

Some will sink by the way and be laid
In the frost of the desolate earth;
And some will return to a maid,
Empty of hand as at birth.

But this out of all will remain,
They have lived and have tossed;
So much in the game will be gain,
Though the gold of the dice has been lost.

CHAPTER XXI

THE RUSH TO ATLIN LAKE

It took me longer to get under way, for I had determined to take at least thirty days' provisions for myself and a newspaper man who joined me here. Our supplies, together with tent, tools, and clothing, made a considerable outfit. However, in a few days we were ready to move, and when I again took my place at the head of a little pack train it seemed quite in the natural order of things.

We left late in the day with intent to camp at the little village of White Pass, which was the end of the wagon road and some twelve miles away. We moved out of town along a road lined with refuse, camp-bottoms, ruined cabins, tin cans, and broken bottles, — all the unsightly débris of the rush of May and June. A part of the way had been corduroyed, for which I was exceedingly grateful, for the Skagway River roared savagely under our feet, while on either side of the roadway at other points I could see abysses of mud which, in the growing darkness, were sufficiently menacing.

Our course was a northerly one. We were ascending the ever narrowing cañon of the river at a gentle grade, with snowy mountains in vista. We arrived at

White Pass at about ten o'clock at night. A little town is springing up there, confident of being an important station on the railroad which was already built to that point.

Thus far the journey had been easy and simple, but immediately after leaving White Pass we entered upon an exceedingly stony road, filled with sharp rock which had been blasted from the railway above us. Upon reaching the end of the wagon road, and entering upon the trail, we came upon the Way of Death. The waters reeked with carrion. The breeze was the breath of carrion, and all nature was made indecent and disgusting by the presence of carcasses. Within the distance of fifteen miles we passed more than two thousand dead horses. It was a cruel land, a land filled with the record of men's merciless greed. Nature herself was cold, majestic, and grand. The trail rough, hard, and rocky. The horses labored hard under their heavy burdens, though the floor they trod was always firm.

Just at the summit in the gray mist, where a bulbous granite ridge cut blackly and lonesomely against the sky, we overtook a flock of turkeys being driven by a one-armed man with a singularly appropriate Scotch cap on his head. The birds sat on the bleak gray rocks in the gathering dusk with the suggestion of being utterly at the end of the world. Their feathers were blown awry by the merciless wind and they looked weary, disconsolate, and bewildered. Their faint, sad gobbling was like the talk of sick people lost in a desert. They were on their way to Dawson City to their death and they seemed to know it.

We camped at the Halfway House, a big tent surrounded by the most diabolical landscape of high peaks lost in mist, with near-by slopes of gray rocks scantily covered with yellow-green grass. All was bare, wild, desolate, and drear. The wind continued to whirl down over the divide, carrying torn gray masses of vapor which cast a gloomy half light across the gruesome little meadow covered with rotting carcasses and crates of bones which filled the air with odor of disease and death.

Within the tent, which flopped and creaked in the wind, we huddled about the cook-stove in the light of a lantern, listening to the loud talk of a couple of packers who were discussing their business with enormous enthusiasm. Happily they grew sleepy at last and peace settled upon us. I unrolled my sleeping bag and slept dreamlessly until the " Russian nobleman," who did the cooking, waked me.

Morning broke bleak and desolate. Mysterious clouds which hid the peaks were still streaming wildly down the cañon. We got away at last, leaving behind us that sad little meadow and its gruesome lakes, and began the slow and toilsome descent over slippery ledges of rock, among endless rows of rotting carcasses, over poisonous streams and through desolate, fire-marked, and ghastly forests of small pines. Everywhere were the traces of the furious flood of humankind that had broken over this height in the early spring. Wreckage of sleighs, abandoned tackle, heaps of camp refuse, clothing, and most eloquent of all the pathway itself, worn

P

into the pitiless iron ledges, made it possible for me to realize something of the scene.

Down there in the gully, on the sullen drift of snow, the winter trail could still be seen like an unclean ribbon and here, where the shrivelled hides of horses lay thick, wound the summer pathway. Up yonder summit, lock-stepped like a file of convicts, with tongues protruding and breath roaring from their distended throats, thousands of men had climbed with killing burdens on their backs, mad to reach the great inland river and the gold belt. Like the men of the Long Trail, they, too, had no time to find the gold under their feet.

It was terrible to see how on every slippery ledge the ranks of horses had broken like waves to fall in heaps like rows of seaweed, tumbled, contorted, and grinning. Their dried skins had taken on the color of the soil, so that I sometimes set foot upon them without realizing what they were. Many of them had saddles on and nearly all had lead-ropes. Some of them had even been tied to trees and left to starve.

In all this could be read the merciless greed and impracticability of these goldseekers. Men who had never driven a horse in their lives, and had no idea what an animal could do, or what he required to eat, loaded their outfits upon some poor patient beast and drove him without feed until, weakened and insecure of foot, he slipped and fell on some one of these cruel ledges of flinty rock.

The business of packing, however, had at last fallen into less cruel or at least more judicial hands, and though the trail was filled with long pack trains going and coming, they were for the most part well taken care of. We met many long trains of packhorses returning empty from Bennett Lake. They were followed by shouting drivers who clattered along on packhorses wherever the trail would permit.

One train carried four immense trunks — just behind the trunks, mounted astride of one of the best horses, rode a bold-faced, handsome white woman followed by a huge negress. The white woman had made her pile by dancing a shameless dance in the dissolute dens of Dawson City, and was on her way to Paris or New York for a "good time." The reports of the hotel keepers made her out to be unspeakably vile. The negress was quite decent by contrast.

At Log Cabin we came in sight of the British flag which marks the boundary line of United States territory, where a camp of mounted police and the British customs officer are located. It was a drear season even in midsummer, a land of naked ledges and cold white peaks. A few small pine trees furnished logs for the cabins and wood for their fires. The government offices were located in tents.

I found the officers most courteous, and the customs fair. The treatment given me at Log Cabin was in marked contrast with the exactions of my own government at Wrangell. All goods were unloaded before the inspector's tent and quickly examined. The miner suffered very little delay.

A number of badly maimed packhorses were running

about on the American side. I was told that the police had stopped them by reason of their sore backs. If a man came to the line with horses overloaded or suffering, he was made to strip the saddles from their backs.

"You can't cross this line with animals like that," was the stern sentence in many cases. This humanity, as unexpected as it was pleasing, deserves the best word of praise of which I am capable.

At last we left behind us all these wrecks of horse-flesh, these poisonous streams, and came down upon Lake Bennett, where the water was considered safe to drink, and where the eye could see something besides death-spotted ledges of savage rocks.

The town was a double row of tents, and log huts set close to the beach whereon boats were building and saws and hammers were uttering a cheerful chorus. Long trains of packhorses filled the streets. The wharfs swarmed with men loading chickens, pigs, vegetables, furniture, boxes of dry-goods, stoves, and every other conceivable domestic utensil into big square barges, which were rigged with tall strong masts bearing most primitive sails. It was a busy scene, but of course very quiet as compared with the activity of May, June, and July.

These barges appealed to me very strongly. They were in some cases floating homes, a combination of mover's wagon and river boat. Many of them contained women and children, with accompanying cats and canary birds. In every face was a look of exultant faith in the venture. They were bound for Dawson City.

The men for Atlin were setting forth in rowboats, or were waiting for the little steamers which had begun to ply between Bennett City and the new gold fields.

I set my little tent, which was about as big as a dog kennel, and crawled into it early, in order to be shielded from the winds, which grew keen as sword blades as the sun sank behind the western mountains. The sky was like November, and I wondered where Burton was encamped. I would have given a great deal to have had him with me on this trip.

THE COAST RANGE OF ALASKA

The wind roars up from the angry sea
With a message of warning and haste to me.
It bids me go where the asters blow,
And the sun-flower waves in the sunset glow.
From the granite mountains the glaciers crawl,
In snow-white spray the waters fall.
The bay is white with the crested waves,
And ever the sea wind ramps and raves.

I hate this cold, bleak northern land,
I fear its snow-flecked harborless strand —
I fly to the south as a homing dove,
Back to the land of corn I love.
And never again shall I set my feet
Where the snow and the sea and the mountains meet.

CHAPTER XXII

THERE is nothing drearier than camping on the edge of civilization like this, where one is surrounded by ill smells, invaded by streams of foul dust, and deprived of wood and clear water. I was exceedingly eager to get away, especially as the wind continued cold and very searching. It was a long dull day of waiting.

At last the boat came in and we trooped aboard — a queer mixture of men and bundles. The boat itself was a mere scow with an upright engine in the centre and a stern-wheel tacked on the outside. There were no staterooms, of course, and almost no bunks. The interior resembled a lumberman's shanty.

We moved off towing a big scow laden with police supplies for Tagish House. The wind was very high and pushed steadily behind, or we would not have gone faster than a walk. We had some eight or ten passengers, all bound for the new gold fields, and these together with their baggage and tools filled the boat to the utmost corner. The feeling of elation among these men reminded me of the great land boom of Dakota in 1883, in which I took a part. There was something fine and free and primitive in it all.

217

We cooked our supper on the boat's stove, furnishing our own food from the supplies we were taking in with us. The ride promised to be very fine. We made off down the narrow lake, which lies between two walls of high bleak mountains, but far in the distance more alluring ranges arose. There was no sign of mineral in the near-by peaks.

Late in the afternoon the wind became so high and the captain of our boat so timid, we were forced to lay by for the night and so swung around under a point, seeking shelter from the wind, which became each moment more furious. I made my bed down on the roof of the boat and went to sleep looking at the drifting clouds overhead. Once or twice during the night when I awoke I heard the howling blast sweeping by with increasing power.

All the next day we loitered on Bennett Lake — the wind roaring without ceasing, and the white-caps running like hares. We drifted at last into a cove and there lay in shelter till six o'clock at night. The sky was clear and the few clouds were gloriously bright and cool and fleecy.

We met several canoes of goldseekers on their return who shouted doleful warnings at us and cursed the worthlessness of the district to which we were bound. They all looked exceedingly dirty, ragged, and sour of visage. At the same time, however, boat after boat went sailing down past us on their way to Atlin and Dawson. They drove straight before the wind, and for the most part experienced little danger, all of which seemed to us to emphasize the unnecessary timidity of our own captain.

There was a charm in this wild spot, but we were too impatient to enjoy it. There were men on board who felt that they were being cheated of a chance to get a gold mine, and when the wind began to fall we fired up and started down the lake. As deep night came on I made my bed on the roof again and went to sleep with the flying sparks lining the sky overhead. I was in some danger of being set on fire, but I preferred sleeping there to sleeping on the floor inside the boat, where the reek of tobacco smoke was sickening.

When I awoke we were driving straight up Tagish Lake, a beautiful, clear, green and blue spread of rippling water with lofty and boldly outlined peaks on each side. The lake ran from southeast to northwest and was much larger than any map shows. We drove steadily for ten hours up this magnificent water with ever increasing splendor of scenery, arriving about sunset at Taku City, which we found to be a little group of tents at the head of Taku arm.

Innumerable boats of every design fringed the shore. Men were coming and men were going, producing a bewildering clash of opinions with respect to the value of the mines. A few of these to whom we spoke said, "It's all a fake," and others were equally certain it was "All right."

A short portage was necessary to reach Atlin Lake, and taking a part of our baggage upon our shoulders we hired the remainder packed on horses and within an hour were moving up the smooth path under the small black pines, across the low ridge which separates the two lakes. At the top of this ridge we were able to look out over the magnificent spread of Atlin Lake, which was more beautiful in every way than Tagish or Taku. It is, in fact, one of the most beautiful lakes I have ever seen.

Far to the southeast it spread until it was lost to view among the bases of the gigantic glacier-laden mountains of the coast range. To the left — that is to the north — it seemed to divide, enclosing a splendid dome-shaped solitary mountain, one fork moving to the east, the other to the west. Its end could not be determined by the eye in either direction. Its width was approximately about ten miles.

At the end of the trail we found an enterprising Canadian with a naphtha launch ready to ferry us across to Atlin City, but were forced to wait for some one who had gone back to Taku for a second load.

While we were waiting, the engineer, who was a round-faced and rather green boy, fell under the influences of a large, plump, and very talkative lady who made the portage just behind us. She so absorbed and fascinated the lad that he let the engine run itself into some cramp of piston or wheel. There was a sudden crunching sound and the propeller stopped. The boy minimized the accident, but the captain upon arrival told us it would be necessary to unload from the boat while the engine was being repaired.

It was now getting dark, and as it was pretty evident that the repairs on the boat would take a large part of the night, we camped where we were. The talkative lady, whom the irreverent called "the glass front," occupied a tent which belonged to the captain of the launch and the rest of us made our beds down under the big trees.

A big fire was built and around this we sat, doing more or less talking. There was an old Tennesseean in the party from Dawson, who talked interminably. He told us of his troubles, trials, and victories in Dawson: how he had been successful, how he had fallen ill, and how his life had been saved by a good old miner who gave him an opportunity to work over his dump. Sick as he was he was able in a few days to find gold enough to take him out of the country to a doctor. He was now on his way back to his claim and professed to be very sceptical of Atlin and every other country except Dawson.

The plump lady developed exceedingly kittenish manners late in the evening, and invited the whole company to share her tent. A singular type of woman, capable of most ladylike manners and having astonishingly sensible moments, but inexpressibly silly most of the time. She was really a powerful, self-confident, and shrewd woman, but preferred to seem young and helpless. Altogether the company was sufficiently curious. There was a young civil engineer from New York City, a land boomer from Skagway, an Irishman from Juneau, a representative of a New York paper, one or two nondescripts from the States, and one or two prospectors from Quebec. The night was cold and beautiful and my partner and I, by going sufficiently far away from the old Tennesseean and the plump lady, were able to sleep soundly until sunrise.

The next morning we hired a large unpainted skiff and by working very hard ourselves in addition to paying full fare we reached camp at about ten o'clock in the morning.   Atlin City was also a clump of tents half hidden in the trees on the beach of the lake near the mouth of Pine Creek.   The lake was surpassingly beautiful under the morning sun.

A crowd of sullen, profane, and grimy men were lounging around, cursing the commissioners and the police.   The beach was fringed with rowboats and canoes, like a New England fishing village, and all day long men were loading themselves into these boats, hungry, tired, and weary, hastening back to Skagway or the coast; while others, fresh, buoyant, and hopeful, came gliding in.

To those who came, the sullen and disappointed ones who were about to go uttered approbrious cries : "See the damn fools come !   What d'you think you're doin' ? On a fishin' excursion ? "

We went into camp on the water front, and hour after hour men laden with packs tramped ceaselessly to and fro along the pathway just below our door.   I was now chief cook and bottle washer, my partner, who was entirely unaccustomed to work of this kind, having the status of a boarder.

The lake was a constant joy to us.   As the sun sank the glacial mountains to the southwest became most royal in their robes of purple and silver.   The sky filled with crimson and saffron clouds which the lake reflected like a mirror. The little rocky islands drowsed in the mist like some strange monsters sleeping on the bosom of the water. The men were filthy and profane for the most part, and made enjoyment of nature almost impossible. Many of them were of the rudest and most uninteresting types, nomads — almost tramps. They had nothing of the epic qualities which belong to the mountaineers and natural miners of the Rocky Mountains. Many of them were loafers and ne'er-do-wells from Skagway and other towns of the coast.

We had a gold pan, a spade, and a pick. Therefore early the next morning we flung a little pack of grub over our shoulders and set forth to test the claims which were situated upon Pine Creek, a stream which entered Lake Atlin near the camp. It was said to be eighteen miles long and Discovery claim was some eight miles up.

We traced our way up the creek as far as Discovery and back, panning dirt at various places with resulting colors in some cases. The trail was full of men racking to and fro with heavy loads on their backs. They moved in little trains of four or five or six men, some going out of the country, others coming in — about an equal number each way. Everything along the creek was staked, and our test work resulted in nothing more than gaining information with regard to what was going on.

The camps on the hills at night swarmed with men in hot debate. The majority believed the camps to be a failure, and loud discussions resounded from the trees as partner and I sat at supper. The town-site men were very nervous. The camps were decreasing in population, and the tone was one of general foreboding.

The campfires flamed all along the lake walk, and the talk of each group could be overheard by any one who listened. Altercations went on with clangorous fury. Almost every party was in division. Some enthusiastic individual had made a find, or had seen some one else who had. His cackle reached other groups, and out of the dark hulking figures loomed to listen or to throw in hot missiles of profanity. Phrases multiplied, mingling inextricably.

" Morgan claims thirty cents to the pan .... good creek claim .... his sluice is about ready .... a clean-up last night .... I don't believe it .... No, Sir, I wouldn't give a hundred dollars for the whole damn moose pasture.... Well, it's good enough for me .... I tell you it's rotten, the whole damn cheese .... You've got to stand in with the police or you can't get .... " and so on and on unendingly, without coherence. I went to sleep only when the sound of the wordy warfare died away.

I permitted myself a day of rest. Borrowing a boat next day, we went out upon the water and up to the mouth of Pine Creek, where we panned some dirt to amuse ourselves. The lake was like liquid glass, the bottom visible at an enormous depth. It made me think of the marvellous water of McDonald Lake in the Kalispels. I steered the boat (with a long-handled spade) and so was able to look about me and absorb at ease the wonderful beauty of this unbroken and unhewn wilderness. The clouds were resplendent, and in every direction the lake vistas were ideally beautiful and constantly changing.

Toward night the sky grew thick and heavy with clouds. The water of the lake was like molten jewels, ruby and amethyst. The boat seemed floating in some strange, ethereal substance hitherto unknown to man — translucent and iridescent. The mountains loomed like dim purple pillars at the western gate of the world, and the rays of the half-hidden sun plunging athwart these sentinels sank deep into the shining flood. Later the sky cleared, and the inverted mountains in the lake were scarcely less vivid than those which rose into the sky.

The next day I spent with gold pan and camera, working my way up Spruce Creek, a branch of Pine. I found men cheerily at work getting out sluice boxes and digging ditches. I panned everywhere, but did not get much in the way of colors, but the creek seemed to grow better as I went up, and promised very rich returns. I came back rushing, making five miles just inside an hour, hungry and tired.

The crowded camp thinned out. The faint-hearted ones who had no courage to sweat for gold sailed away. Others went out upon their claims to build cabins and lay sluices. I found them whip-sawing lumber, building cabins, and digging ditches. Each day the news grew more encouraging, each day brought the discovery of a new creek or a lake. Men came back in swarms and reporting finds on " Lake Surprise," a newly discovered big body of water, and at last came the report of surprising discoveries in the benches high above the creek.

Q

In the camp one night I heard a couple of men talking around a campfire near me. One of them said: "Why, you know old Sperry was digging on the ridge just above Discovery and I came along and see him up there. And I said, 'Hullo, uncle, what you doin', diggin' your grave?' And the old feller said, 'You just wait a few minutes and I'll show ye.' Well, sir, he filled up a sack o' dirt and toted it down to the creek, and I went along with him to see him wash it out, and say, he took $3.25 out of one pan of that dirt, and $1.85 out of the other pan. Well, that knocked me. I says, 'Uncle, you're all right.' And then I made tracks for a bench claim next him. Well, about that time everybody began to hustle for bench claims, and now you can't get one anywhere near him."

At another camp, a packer was telling of an immense nugget that had been discovered somewhere on the upper waters of Birch Creek. "And say, fellers, you know there is another lake up there pretty near as big as Atlin. They are calling it Lake Surprise. I heard a feller say a few days ago there was a big lake up there and I thought he meant a lake six or eight miles long. On the very high ground next to Birch, you can look down over that lake and I bet it's sixty miles long. It must reach nearly to Teslin Lake." There was something pretty fine in the thought of being in a country where lakes sixty miles long were being discovered and set forth on the maps of the world. Up to this time Atlin Lake itself was unmapped. To an unpractical man like myself it was reward enough to feel the thrill of excitement which comes with such discoveries.

However, I was not a goldseeker, and when I determined to give up any further pursuit of mining and to delegate it entirely to my partner, I experienced a feeling of relief. I determined to " stick to my last," notwithstanding the fascination which I felt in the sight of placer gold. Quartz mining has never had the slightest attraction for me, but to see the gold washed out of the sand, to see it appear bright and shining in the black sand in the bottom of the pan, is really worth while. It is first-hand contact with Nature's stores of wealth.

I went up to Discovery for the last time with my camera slung over my shoulder, and my note-book in hand to take a final survey of the miners and to hear for the last time their exultant talk. I found them exceedingly cheerful, even buoyant.

The men who had gone in with ten days' provisions, the tender-foot miners, the men " with a cigarette and a sandwich," had gone out. Those who remained were men who knew their business and were resolute and self-sustaining.

There was a crowd of such men around the land-office tents and many filings were made. Nearly every man had his little phial of gold to show. No one was loud, but every one seemed to be quietly confident and replied to my questions in a low voice, " Well, you can safely say the country is all right."

The day was fine like September in Wisconsin. The lake as I walked back to it was very alluring. My mind returned again and again to the things I had left behind for so long. My correspondence, my books, my friends, all the literary interests of my life, began to reassert their dominion over me. For some time I had realized that this was almost an ideal spot for camping or mining. Just over in the wild country toward Teslin Lake, herds of caribou were grazing. Moose and bear were being killed daily, rich and unknown streams were waiting for the gold pan, the pick and the shovel, but — it was not for me! I was ready to return — eager to return.

THE FREEMAN OF THE HILLS

I have no master but the wind,
    My only liege the sun;
All bonds and ties I leave behind,
    Free as the wolf I run.
My master wind is passionless,
    He neither chides nor charms;
He fans me or he freezes me,
    And helps are quick as harms.

He never turns to injure me,
    And when his voice is high
I crouch behind a rock and see
    His storm of snows go by.
He too is subject of the sun,
    As all things earthly are,
Where'er he flies, where'er I run,
    We know our kingly star.

THE VOICE OF THE MAPLE TREE

I am worn with the dull-green spires of fir,
I am tired of endless talk of gold,
I long for the cricket's cheery whirr,
And the song that the maples sang of old.
O the beauty and learning and light
That lie in the leaves of the level lands !
They shake my heart in the deep of the night,
They call me and bless me with calm, cool hands.

> *Sing, O leaves of the maple tree,*
> *I hear your voice by the savage sea,*
> *Hear and hasten to home and thee !*

CHAPTER XXIII

THE END OF THE TRAIL

THE day on which I crossed the lake to Taku City was most glorious. A September haze lay on the mountains, whose high slopes, orange, ruby, and golden-green, allured with almost irresistible attraction. Although the clouds were gathering in the east, the sunset was superb. Taku arm seemed a river of gold sweeping between gates of purple. As the darkness came on, a long creeping line of fire crept up a near-by mountain's side, and from time to time, as it reached some great pine, it flamed to the clouds like a mighty geyser of red-hot lava. It was splendid but terrible to witness.

The next day was a long, long wait for the steamer. I now had in my pocket just twelve dollars, but possessed a return ticket on one of the boats. This ticket was not good on any other boat, and naturally I felt considerable anxiety for fear it would not turn up. My dinner consisted of moose steak, potatoes, and bread, and was most thoroughly enjoyed.

At last the steamer came, but it was not the one on which I had secured passage, and as it took almost my last dollar to pay for deck passage thereon, I lived on some small cakes of my own baking, which I carried in a bag. I was now in a sad predicament unless I should connect at Lake Bennett with some one who would carry my outfit back to Skagway on credit. I ate my stale cakes and drank lake water, and thus fooled the little Jap steward out of two dollars. It was a sad business, but unavoidable.

The lake being smooth, the trip consumed but thirteen hours, and we arrived at Bennett Lake late at night. Hoisting my bed and luggage to my shoulder, I went up on the side-hill like a stray dog, and made my bed down on the sand beside a cart, near a shack. The wind, cold and damp, swept over the mountains with a roar. I was afraid the owners of the cart might discover me there, and order me to seek a bed elsewhere. Dogs sniffed around me during the night, but on the whole I slept very well. I could feel the sand blowing over me in the wild gusts of wind which relented not in all my stay at Bennett City.

I spent literally the last cent I had on a scanty breakfast, and then, in company with Doctor G. (a fellow prospector), started on my return to the coast over the far-famed Chilcoot Pass.

At 9 A.M. we took the little ferry for the head of Lindernan Lake. The doctor paid my fare. The boat, a wabbly craft, was crowded with returning Klondikers, many of whom were full of importance and talk of their wealth; while others, sick and worn, with a wistful gleam in their eyes, seemed eager to get back to civilization and medical care. There were some women, also, who had made a fortune in dance-houses and were now bound for New York and Paris, where dresses could be had in the latest styles and in any quantities.

My travelling mate, the doctor, was a tall and vigorous man from Winnipeg, accustomed to a plainsman's life, hardy and resolute. He said, "We ought to make Dyea to-day." I said in reply, "Very well, we can try."

It was ten o'clock when we left the little boat and hit the trail, which was thirty miles long, and passed over the summit three thousand six hundred feet above the sea. The doctor's pace was tremendous, and we soon left every one else behind.

I carried my big coat and camera, which hindered me not a little. For the first part of the journey the doctor preceded me, his broad shoulders keeping off the powerful wind and driving mist, which grew thicker as we rose among the ragged cliffs beside a roaring stream.

That walk was a grim experience. Until two o'clock we climbed resolutely along a rough, rocky, and wooded trail, with the heavy mist driving into our faces. The road led up a rugged cañon and over a fairly good wagon road until somewhere about twelve o'clock. Then the foot trail deflected to the left, and climbed sharply over slippery ledges, along banks of ancient snows in which carcasses of horses lay embedded, and across many rushing little streams. The way grew grimmer each step. At last we came to Crater Lake, and from that point on it was a singular and sinister land of grassless crags swathed in mist. Nothing could be seen at this point but a desolate, flat expanse of barren sands over which gray-green streams wandered in confusion, coming from darkness and vanishing in obscurity. Strange shapes showed in the gray dusk of the Crater. It was like a landscape in hell. It seemed to be the end of the earth, where no life had ever been or could long exist.

Across this flat to its farther wall we took our way, facing the roaring wind now heavy with clouds of rain. At last we stood in the mighty notch of the summit, through which the wind rushed as though hurrying to some far-off, deep-hidden vacuum in the world. The peaks of the mountains were lost in clouds out of which water fell in vicious slashes.

The mist set the imagination free. The pinnacles around us were like those which top the Valley of Desolation. We seemed each moment about to plunge into ladderless abysses. Nothing ever imagined by Poe or Doré could be more singular, more sinister, than these summits in such a light, in such a storm. It might serve as the scene for an exiled devil. The picture of Beelzebub perched on one of those gray, dimly seen crags, his form outlined in the mist, would shake the heart. I thought of "Peer Gynt" wandering in the high home of the Trolls. Crags beetled beyond crags, and nothing could be heard but the wild waters roaring in the obscure depths beneath our feet. There was no sky, no level place, no growing thing, no bird or beast, — only crates of bones to show where some heartless master had pushed a faithful horse up these terrible heights to his death.

And here — just here in a world of crags and mist — I heard a shout of laughter, and then bursting upon my sight, strong-limbed, erect, and full-bosomed, appeared a girl. Her face was like a rain-wet rose — a splendid, unexpected flower set in this dim and gray and desolate place. Fearlessly she fronted me to ask the way, a laugh upon her lips, her big gray eyes confident of man's chivalry, modest and sincere. I had been so long among rude men and their coarse consorts that this fair woman lit the mist as if with sudden sunshine — just a moment and was gone. There were others with her, but they passed unnoticed. There in the gloom, like a stately pink rose, I met the Girl of the Mist.

Sheep Camp was the end of the worst portion of the trail. I had now crossed both the famed passes, much improved of course. They are no longer dangerous (a woman in good health can cross them easily), but they are grim and grievous ways. They reek of cruelty and every association that is coarse and hard. They possess a peculiar value to me in that they throw into fadeless splendor the wealth, the calm, the golden sunlight which lay upon the proud beauty of Atlin Lake.

The last hours of the trip formed a supreme test of endurance. At Sheep Camp, a wet and desolate shanty town, eight miles from Dyea, we came upon stages just starting over our road. But as they were all open carriages, and we were both wet with perspiration and rain, and hungry and tired, we refused to book passage.

"To ride eight miles in an open wagon would mean a case of pneumonia to me," I said.

"Quite right," said the doctor, and we pulled out down the road at a smart clip.

The rain had ceased, but the air was raw and the sky gray, and I was very tired, and those eight miles stretched out like a rubber string. Night fell before we had passed over half the road, which lay for the most part down the flat along the Chilcoot River. In fact, we crossed this stream again and again. In places there were bridges, but most of the crossings were fords where it was necessary to wade through the icy water above our shoe tops. Our legs, numb and weary, threw off this chill with greater pain each time. As the night fell we could only see the footpath by the dim shine of its surface patted smooth by the moccasined feet of the Indian packers. At last I walked with a sort of mechanical action which was dependent on my subconscious will. There was nothing else to do but to go through. The doctor was a better walker than I. His long legs had more reach as well as greater endurance. Nevertheless he admitted being about as tired as ever in his life.

At last, when it seemed as though I could not wade any more of those icy streams and continue to walk, we came in sight of the electric lights on the wharfs of Dyea, sparkling like jewels against the gray night. Their radiant promise helped over the last mile miraculously. We were wet to the knees and covered with mud as we entered upon the straggling street of the decaying town. We stopped in at the first restaurant to get something hot to eat, but found ourselves almost too tired to enjoy even pea soup. But it warmed us up a little, and keeping on down the street we came at last to a hotel of very comfortable accommodations. We ordered a fire built to dry our clothing, and staggered up the stairs.

That ended the goldseekers' trail for me. Henceforward I intended to ride — nevertheless I was pleased to think I could still walk thirty miles in eleven hours through a rain storm, and over a summit three thousand six hundred feet in height. The city had not entirely eaten the heart out of my body.

We arose from a dreamless sleep, somewhat sore, but in amazingly good trim considering our condition the night before, and made our way into our muddy clothing with grim resolution. After breakfast we took a small steamer which ran to Skagway, where we spent the day arranging to take the steamer to the south. We felt quite at home in Skagway now, and Chicago seemed not very far away. Having made connection with my bankers I stretched out in my twenty-five cent bunk with the assurance of a gold king.

Here the long trail took a turn. I had been among the miners and hunters for four months. I had been one of them. I had lived the essentials of their lives, and had been able to catch from them some hint of their outlook on life. They were a disappointment to me in some ways. They seemed like mechanisms. They moved as if drawn by some great magnet whose centre was Dawson City. They appeared to drift on and in toward that human maelstrom going irresolutely to their ruin. They did not seem to me strong men — on the contrary, they seemed weak men — or men strong with one insane purpose. They set their faces toward the golden north, and went on and on through every obstacle like men dreaming, like somnambulists — bending their backs to the most crushing burdens, their faces distorted with effort. "On to Dawson!" "To the Klondike!" That was all they knew.

I overtook them in the Fraser River Valley, I found them in Hazleton. They were setting sail at Bennett, tugging oars on the Hotalinqua, and hundreds of them were landing every day at Dawson, there to stand with lax jaws waiting for something to turn up — lost among thousands of their kind swarming in with the same insane purpose.

Skagway was to me a sad place. On either side rose green mountains covered with crawling glaciers. Between these stern walls, a cold and violent wind roared ceaselessly from the sea gates through which the ships drive hurriedly. All these grim presences depressed me. I longed for release from them. I waited with impatience the coming of the steamer which was to rescue me from the merciless beach.

At last it came, and its hoarse boom thrilled the heart of many a homesick man like myself. We had not much to put aboard, and when I climbed the gang-plank it was with a feeling of fortunate escape.

A GIRL ON THE TRAIL

A flutter of skirts in the dapple of leaves on the trees,
The sound of a small, happy voice on the breeze,
The print of a slim little foot on the trail,
And the miners rejoice as they hammer with picks in
      the vale.

For fairer than gold is the face of a maid,
And sovereign as stars the light of her eyes;
For women alone were the long trenches laid;
For women alone they defy the stern skies.

These toilers are grimy, and hairy, and dun
With the wear of the wind, the scorch of the sun;
But their picks fall slack, their foul tongues are mute —
As the maiden goes by these earthworms salute!

CHAPTER XXIV

THE steamer was crowded with men who had also made the turn at the end of the trail. There were groups of prospectors (disappointed and sour) from Copper River, where neither copper nor gold had been found. There were miners sick and broken who had failed on the Tanana, and others, emaciated and eager-eyed, from Dawson City going out with a part of the proceeds of the year's work to see their wives and children. There were a few who considered themselves great capitalists, and were on their way to spend the winter in luxury in the Eastern cities, and there were grub stakers who had squandered their employers' money in drink and gaming.

None of them interested me very greatly. I was worn out with the filth and greed and foolishness of many of these men. They were commonplace citizens, turned into stampeders without experience or skill.

One of the most successful men on the boat had been a truckman in the streets of Tacoma, and was now the silly possessor of a one-third interest in some great mines on the Klondike River. He told every one of his great deeds, and what he was worth. . He let us

R   241

know how big his house was, and how much he paid for his piano. He was not a bad man, he was merely a cheap man, and was followed about by a gang of heelers to whom drink was luxury and vice an entertainment. These parasites slapped the teamster on the shoulder and listened to every empty phrase he uttered, as though his gold had made of him something sacred and omniscient.

I had no interest in him till being persuaded to play the fiddle he sat in the " social room," and sawed away on " Honest John," " The Devil's Dream," " Haste to the Wedding," and " The Fisher's Hornpipe." He lost all sense of being a millionnaire, and returned to his simple, unsophisticated self. The others cheered him because he had gold. I cheered him because he was a good old " corduroy fiddler."

Again we passed between the lofty blue-black and bronze-green walls of Lynn Canal. The sea was cold, placid, and gray. The mist cut the mountains at the shoulder. Vast glaciers came sweeping down from the dread mystery of the upper heights. Lower still lines of running water white as silver came leaping down from cliff to cliff — slender, broken line, nearly perpendicular — to fall at last into the gray hell of the sea.

It was a sullen land which menaced as with lowering brows and clenched fists. A landscape without delicacy of detail or warmth or variety of color — a land demanding young, cheerful men. It was no place for the old or for women.

As we neared Wrangell the next afternoon I tackled

the purser about carrying my horse. He had no room, so I left the boat in order to wait for another with better accommodations for Ladrone.

Almost the first man I met on the wharf was Donald.

"How's the horse?" I queried.

"Gude! — fat and sassy. There's no a fence in a' the town can hold him. He jumped into Colonel Crittendon's garden patch, and there's a dollar to pay for the cauliflower he ate, and he broke down a fence by the church, ye've to fix that up — but he's in gude trim himsel'."

"Tell 'm to send in their bills," I replied with vast relief. "Has he been much trouble to you?"

"Verra leetle except to drive into the lot at night. I had but to go down where he was feeding and soon as he heard me comin' he made for the lot — he knew quite as well as I did what was wanted of him. He's a canny old boy."

As I walked out to find the horse I discovered his paths everywhere. He had made himself entirely at home. He owned the village and was able to walk any sidewalk in town. Everybody knew his habits. He drank in a certain place, and walked a certain round of daily feeding. The children all cried out at me: "Goin' to find the horsie? He's over by the church." A darky woman smiled from the door of a cabin and said, "You ole hoss lookin' mighty fine dese days."

When I came to him I was delighted and amused. He had taken on some fat and a great deal of dirt. He had also acquired an aldermanic paunch which quite destroyed his natural symmetry of body, but he was well and strong and lively. He seemed to recognize me, and as I put the rope about his neck and fell to in the effort to make him clean once more, he seemed glad of my presence.

That day began my attempt to get away. I carted out my feed and saddles, and when all was ready I sat on the pier and watched the burnished water of the bay for the dim speck which a steamer makes in rounding the distant island. At last the cry arose, " A steamer from the north! " I hurried for Ladrone, and as I passed with the horse the citizens smiled incredulously and asked, " Goin' to take the horse with you, eh ? "

The boys and girls came out to say good-by to the horse on whose back they had ridden. Ladrone followed me most trustfully, looking straight ahead, his feet clumping loudly on the boards of the walk. Hitching him on the wharf I lugged and heaved and got everything in readiness.

In vain! The steamer had no place for my horse and I was forced to walk him back and turn him loose once more upon the grass. I renewed my watching. The next steamer did not touch at the same wharf. Therefore I carted all my goods, feed, hay, and general plunder, around to the other wharf. As I toiled to and fro the citizens began to smile very broadly. I worked like a hired man in harvest. At last, horse, feed, and baggage were once more ready. When the next boat came in I timidly approached the purser.

No, he had no place for me but would take my

horse ! Once more I led Ladrone back to pasture and the citizens laughed most unconcealedly. They laid bets on my next attempt. In McKinnon's store I was greeted as a permanent citizen of Fort Wrangell. I began to grow nervous on my own account. Was I to remain forever in Wrangell? The bay was most beautiful, but the town was wretched. It became each day more unendurable to me. I searched the waters of the bay thereafter, with gaze that grew really anxious. I sat for hours late at night holding my horse and glaring out into the night in the hope to see the lights of a steamer appear round the high hills of the coast.

At last the *Forallen*, a great barnyard of a ship, came in. I met the captain. I paid my fare. I got my contract and ticket, and leading Ladrone into the hoisting box I stepped aside.

The old boy was quiet while I stood near, but when the whistle sounded and the sling rose in air leaving me below, his big eyes flashed with fear and dismay. He struggled furiously for a moment and then was quiet. A moment later he dropped into the hold and was safe. He thought himself in a barn once more, and when I came hurrying down the stairway he whinnied. He seized the hay I put before him and thereafter was quite at home.

The steamer had a score of mules and work horses on board, but they occupied stalls on the upper deck, leaving Ladrone aristocratically alone in his big, well-ventilated barn, and there three times each day I went to feed and water him. I rubbed him with hay till his coat began to glimmer in the light and planned what I could do to help him through a storm. Fortunately the ocean was perfectly smooth even across the entrance to Queen Charlotte's Sound, where the open sea enters and the big swells are sometimes felt. Ladrone never knew he was moving at all.

The mate of the boat took unusual interest in the horse because of his deeds and my care of him.

Meanwhile I was hearing from time to time of my fellow-sufferers on the Long Trail. It was reported in Wrangell that some of the unfortunates were still on the snowy divide between the Skeena and the Stikeen. That terrible trail will not soon be forgotten by any one who traversed it.

On the fifth day we entered Seattle and once more the sling-box opened its doors for Ladrone. This time he struggled not at all. He seemed to say: " I know this thing. I tried it once and it didn't hurt me — I'm not afraid."

Now this horse belongs to the wild country. He was born on the bunch-grass hills of British Columbia and he had never seen a street-car in his life. Engines he knew something about, but not much. Steamboats and ferries he knew a great deal about; but all the strange monsters and diabolical noises of a city street were new to him, and it was with some apprehension that I took his rein to lead him down to the freight depot and his car.

Again this wonderful horse amazed me. He pointed his alert and quivering ears at me and followed with never so much as a single start or shying bound. He seemed to reason that as I had led him through many dangers safely I could still be trusted. Around us huge trucks rattled, electric cars clanged, railway engines whizzed and screamed, but Ladrone never so much as tightened the rein; and when in the dark of the chute (which led to the door of the car) he put his soft nose against me to make sure I was still with him, my heart grew so tender that I would not have left him behind for a thousand dollars.

I put him in a roomy box-car and bedded him knee-deep in clean yellow straw. I padded the hitching pole with his blanket, moistened his hay, and put some bran before him. Then I nailed him in and took my leave of him with some nervous dread, for the worst part of his journey was before him. He must cross three great mountain ranges and ride eight days, over more than two thousand miles of railway. I could not well go with him, but I planned to overhaul him at Spokane and see how he was coming on.

I did not sleep much that night. I recalled how the great forest trees were blazing last year when I rode over this same track. I thought of the sparks flying from the engine, and how easy it would be for a single cinder to fall in the door and set all that dry straw ablaze. I was tired and my mind conjured up such dire images as men dream of after indigestible dinners.

O THE FIERCE DELIGHT

O the fierce delight, the passion
    That comes from the wild,
Where the rains and the snows go over,
    And man is a child.

Go, set your face to the open,
    And lay your breast to the blast,
When the pines are rocking and groaning,
    And the rent clouds tumble past.

Go swim the streams of the mountains,
    Where the gray-white waters are mad,
Go set your foot on the summit,
    And shout and be glad !

CHAPTER XXV

LADRONE TRAVELS IN STATE

With a little leisure to walk about and talk with the citizens of Seattle, I became aware of a great change since the year before. The boom of the goldseeker was over. The talk was more upon the Spanish war; the business of outfitting was no longer paramount; the reckless hurrah, the splendid exultation, were gone. Men were sailing to the north, but they embarked, methodically, in business fashion.

It is safe to say that the north will never again witness such a furious rush of men as that which took place between August, '97, and June, '98. Gold is still there, and it will continue to be sought, but the attention of the people is directed elsewhere. In Seattle, as all along the line, the talk a year ago had been almost entirely on gold hunting. Every storekeeper advertised Klondike goods, but these signs were now rusty and faded. The fever was over, the reign of the humdrum was restored.

Taking the train next day, I passed Ladrone in the night somewhere, and as I looked from my window at the great fires blazing in the forest, my fear of his burning came upon me again. At Spokane I waited with great anxiety for him to arrive. At last the train drew in and I hurried to his car.   The door was closed, and as I nervously forced it open he whinnied with that glad chuckling a gentle horse uses toward his master.   He had plenty of hay, but was hot and thirsty, and I hurried at risk of life and limb to bring him cool water.   His eyes seemed to shine with delight as he saw me coming with the big bucket of cool drink.   Leaving him a tub of water, I bade him good-by once more and started him for Helena, five hundred miles away.

At Missoula, the following evening, I rushed into the ticket office and shouted, " Where is ' 54 ' ? "

The clerk knew me and smilingly extended his hand.

" How de do ?   She has just pulled out.   The horse is all O K.   We gave him fresh water and feed."

I thanked him and returned to my train.

Reaching Livingston in the early morning I was forced to wait nearly all day for the train.   This was no hardship, however, for it enabled me to return once more to the plain.   All the old familiar presences were there. The splendid sweep of brown, smooth hills, the glory of clear sky, the crisp exhilarating air, appealed to me with great power after my long stay in the cold, green mountains of the north.

I walked out a few miles from the town over the grass brittle and hot, from which the clapping grasshoppers rose in swarms, and dropping down on the point of a mesa I relived again in drowse the joys of other days. It was plain to me that goldseeking in the Rocky Mountains was marvellously simple and easy compared to even the best sections of the Northwest, and the long journey of the Forty-niners was not only incredibly more splendid and dramatic, but had the allurement of a land of eternal summer beyond the final great range. The long trail I had just passed was not only grim and monotonous, but led toward an ever increasing ferocity of cold and darkness to the arctic circle and the silence of death.

When the train came crawling down the pink and purple slopes of the hills at sunset that night, I was ready for my horse. Bridle in hand I raced after the big car while it was being drawn up into the freight yards. As I galloped I held excited controversy with the head brakeman. I asked that the car be sent to the platform. He objected. I insisted and the car was thrown in. I entered, and while Ladrone whinnied glad welcome I knocked out some bars, bridled him, and said, " Come, boy, now for a gambol." He followed me without the slightest hesitation out on the platform and down the steep slope to the ground. There I mounted him without waiting for saddle and away we flew.

He was gay as a bird. His neck arched and his eyes and ears were quick as squirrels. We galloped down to the Yellowstone River and once more he thrust his dusty nozzle deep into the clear mountain water. Then away he raced until our fifteen minutes were up. I was glad to quit. He was too active for me to enjoy riding without a saddle. Right up to the door of the car he trotted, seeming to understand that his journey was not yet finished. He entered unhesitatingly and took his place. I battened down the bars, nailed the doors into place, filled his tub with cold water, mixed him a bran mash, and once more he rolled away. I sent him on this time, however, with perfect confidence. He was actually getting fat on his prison fare, and was too wise to allow himself to be bruised by the jolting of the cars.

The bystanders seeing a horse travelling in such splendid loneliness asked, " Runnin' horse ? " and I (to cover my folly) replied evasively, " He can run a little for good money." This satisfied every one that he was a sprinter and quite explained his private car.

At Bismarck I found myself once more ahead of " 54 " and waited all day for the horse to appear. As the time of the train drew near I borrowed a huge water pail and tugged a supply of water out beside the track and there sat for three hours, expecting the train each moment. At last it came, but Ladrone was not there. His car was missing. I rushed into the office of the operator : " Where's the horse in ' 13,238 ' ? " I asked.

" I don't know," answered the agent, in the tone of one who didn't care.

Visions of Ladrone side-tracked somewhere and perishing for want of air and water filled my mind. I waxed warm.

" That horse must be found at once," I said. The clerks and operators wearily looked out of the window. The idea of any one being so concerned about a horse was to them insanity or worse. I insisted. I banged my fist on the table. At last one of the young men yawned languidly, looked at me with dim eyes, and as one brain-cell coalesced with another seemed to mature an idea. He said : —

"Rheinhart had a horse this morning on his extra."

"Did he — maybe that's the one." They discussed this probability with lazy indifference. At last they condescended to include me in their conversation.

I insisted on their telegraphing till they found that horse, and with an air of distress and saint-like patience the agent wrote out a telegram and sent it. Thereafter he could not see me ; nevertheless I persisted. I returned to the office each quarter of an hour to ask if an answer had come to the telegram. At last it came. Ladrone was ahead and would arrive in St. Paul nearly twelve hours before me. I then telegraphed the officers of the road to see that he did not suffer and composed myself as well as I could for the long wait.

At St. Paul I hurried to the freight office and found the horse had been put in a stable. I sought the stable, and there, among the big dray horses, looking small and trim as a racer, was the lost horse, eating merrily on some good Minnesota timothy. He was just as much at ease there as in the car or the boat or on the marshes of the Skeena valley, but he was still a half-day's ride from his final home.

I bustled about filling up another car. Again for the last time I sweated and tugged getting feed, water, and bedding. Again the railway hands marvelled and looked askance. Again some one said, "Does it pay to bring a horse like that so far ? "

"Pay ! " I shouted, thoroughly disgusted, "does it

pay to feed a dog for ten years? Does it pay to ride a bicycle? Does it pay to bring up a child? Pay — no; it does not pay. I'm amusing myself. You drink beer because you like to, you use tobacco — I squander my money on a horse." I said a good deal more than the case demanded, being hot and dusty and tired and — I had broken loose. The clerk escaped through a side door.

Once more I closed the bars on the gray and saw him wheeled out into the grinding, jolting tangle of cars where the engines cried out like some untamable flesh-eating monsters. The light was falling, the smoke thickening, and it was easy to imagine a tragic fate for the patient and lonely horse.

Delay in getting the car made me lose my train and I was obliged to take a late train which did not stop at my home. I was still paying for my horse out of my own bone and sinew. At last the luscious green hills, the thick grasses, the tall corn-shocks and the portly hay-stacks of my native valley came in view and they never looked so abundant, so generous, so entirely suf-ficing to man and beast as now in returning from a land of cold green forests, sparse grass, and icy streams.

At ten o'clock another huge freight train rolled in, Ladrone's car was side-tracked and sent to the chute. For the last time he felt the jolt of the car. In a few minutes I had his car opened and a plank laid.

" Come, boy ! " I called. " This is home."

He followed me as before, so readily, so trustingly, my heart responded to his affection. I swung to the saddle.

With neck arched high and with a proud and lofty stride he left the door of his prison behind him. His fame had spread through the village. On every corner stood the citizens to see him pass.

As I entered the door to the barn I said to him : —

" Enter ! Your days of thirst, of hunger, of cruel exposure to rain and snow are over. Here is food that shall not fail," and he seemed to understand.

It might seem absurd if I were to give expression to the relief and deep pleasure it gave me to put that horse into that familiar stall. He had been with me more than four thousand miles. He had carried me through hundreds of icy streams and over snow fields. He had responded to every word and obeyed every command. He had suffered from cold and hunger and poison. He had walked logs and wallowed through quicksands. He had helped me up enormous mountains and I had guided him down dangerous declivities. His faithful heart had never failed even in days of direst need, and now he shall live amid plenty and have no care so long as he lives. It does not pay, — that is sure, — but after all what does pay ?

s

THE LURE OF THE DESERT

I lie in my blanket, alone, alone!
Hearing the voice of the roaring rain,
And my heart is moved by the wind's low moan
To wander the wastes of the wind-worn plain,
Searching for something — I cannot tell —
The face of a woman, the love of a child —
Or only the rain-wet prairie swell
Or the savage woodland wide and wild.

I must go away — I know not where!
Lured by voices that cry and cry,
Drawn by fingers that clutch my hair,
Called to the mountains bleak and high,
Led to the mesas hot and bare.
O God! How my heart's blood wakes and thrills
To the cry of the wind, the lure of the hills.
I'll follow you, follow you far;
Ye voices of winds, and rain and sky,
To the peaks that shatter the evening star.
Wealth, honor, wife, child — all
I have in the city's keep,
I loose and forget when ye call and call
And the desert winds around me sweep.

CHAPTER XXVI

THE GOLDSEEKERS REACH THE GOLDEN RIVER

THE goldseekers are still seeking. I withdrew, but they went on. In the warmth and security of my study, surrounded by the peace and comfort of my native Coolly, I thought of them as they went toiling over the trail, still toward the north. It was easy for me to imagine their daily life. The Manchester boys and Burton, my partner, left Glenora with ten horses and more than two thousand pounds of supplies.

Twice each day this immense load had to be handled; sometimes in order to rest and graze the ponies, every sack and box had to be taken down and lifted up to their lashings again four times each day. This meant toil. It meant also constant worry and care while the train was in motion. Three times each day a campfire was built and coffee and beans prepared.

However, the weather continued fair, my partner wrote me, and they arrived at Teslin Lake in September, after being a month on the road, and there set about building a boat to carry them down the river.

Here the horses were sold, and I know it must have been a sad moment for Burton to say good-by to his faithful brutes. But there was no help for it. There was no more thought of going to the head-waters of the Pelly and no more use for the horses.   Indeed, the gold-hunters abandoned all thought of the Nisutlin and the Hotalinqua.   They were fairly in the grasp of the tremendous current which seemed to get ever swifter as it approached the mouth of the Klondike River.   They were mad to reach the pool wherein all the rest of the world was fishing.   Nothing less would satisfy them.

At last they cast loose from the shore and started down the river, straight into the north.   Each hour, each mile, became a menace.   Day by day they drifted while the spitting snows fell hissing into the cold water, and ice formed around the keel of the boat at night. They passed men camped and panning dirt, but continued resolute, halting only "to pass the good word."

It grew cold with appalling rapidity and the sun fell away to the south with desolating speed.   The skies darkened and lowered as the days shortened.   All signs of life except those of other argonauts disappeared.   The river filled with drifting ice, and each night landing became more difficult.

At last the winter came.   The river closed up like an iron trap, and before they knew it they were caught in the jam of ice and fighting for their lives.   They landed on a wooded island after a desperate struggle and went into camp with the thermometer thirty below zero.   But what of that ?   They were now in the gold belt.   After six months of incessant toil, of hope deferred, they were at last on the spot toward which they had struggled.

All around them was the overflow from the Klondike.

Their desire to go farther was checked. They had reached the counter current — the back-water — and were satisfied.

Leaving to others the task of building a permanent camp, my sturdy partner, a couple of days later, started prospecting in company with two others whom he had selected to represent the other outfit. The thermometer was fifty-six degrees below zero, and yet for seven days, with less than six hours' sleep, without a tent, those devoted idiots hunted the sands of a near-by creek for gold, and really staked claims.

On the way back one of the men grew sleepy and would have lain down to die except for the vigorous treatment of Burton, who mauled him and dragged him about and rubbed him with snow until his blood began to circulate once more. In attempting to walk on the river, which was again in motion, Burton fell through, wetting one leg above the knee. It was still more than thirty degrees below zero, but what of that ? He merely kept going.

They reached the bank opposite the camp late on the seventh day, but were unable to cross the moving ice. For the eighth night they " danced around the fire as usual," not daring to sleep for fear of freezing. They literally frosted on one side while scorching at the fire on the other, turning like so many roasting pigs before the blaze. The river solidified during the night and they crossed to the camp to eat and sleep in safety.

A couple of weeks later they determined to move down the river to a new stampede in Thistle Creek.

Once more these indomitable souls left their warm cabin, took up their beds and nearly two thousand pounds of outfit and toiled down the river still farther into the terrible north. The chronicle of this trip by Burton is of mathematical brevity: "On 20th concluded to move. Took four days. Very cold. Ther. down to 45 below. Froze one toe. Got claim — now building cabin. Expect to begin singeing in a few days."

The toil, the suffering, the monotonous food, the lack of fire, he did not dwell upon, but singeing, that is to say burning down through the eternally frozen ground, was to begin at once. To singe a hole into the soil ten or fifteen feet deep in the midst of the sunless severity of the arctic circle is no light task, but these men will do it ; if hardihood and honest toil are of any avail they will all share in the precious sand whose shine has lured them through all the dark days of the long trail, calling with such power that nothing could stay them or turn them aside.

If they fail, well —

> This out of all will remain,
> They have lived and have tossed.
> So much of the game will be gain,
> Though the gold of the dice has been lost.

HERE THE TRAIL ENDS

Here the trail ends — Here by a river
So swifter, and darker, and colder
Than any we crossed on our long, long way.
Steady, Dan, steady.   Ho, there, my dapple,
You first from the saddle shall slip and be free.
Now go, you are clear from command of a master;
Go wade in the grasses, go munch at the grain.
I love you, my faithful, but all is now over;
Ended the comradeship held 'twixt us twain.
I go to the river and the wide lands beyond it,
You go to the pasture, and death claims us all.
For here the trail ends!

Here the trail ends!
Draw near with the broncos.
Slip the hitch, loose the cinches,
Slide the saw-bucks away from each worn, weary back.
We are done with the axe, the camp, and the kettle;
Strike hand to each cayuse and send him away.
Let them go where the roses and grasses are growing,
To the meadows that slope to the warm western sea.
No more shall they serve us; no more shall they suffer
The sting of the lash, the heat of the day.
Soon they will go to a winterless haven,
To the haven of beasts where none may enslave.
For here the trail ends.

Here the trail ends.
Never again shall the far-shining mountains allure us,
No more shall the icy mad torrents appall.
Fold up the sling ropes, coil down the cinches,
Cache the saddles, and put the brown bridles away.
Not one of the roses of Navajo silver,
Not even a spur shall we save from the rust.
Put away the worn tent-cloth, let the red people have it;
We are done with all shelter, we are done with the gun.
Not so much as a pine branch, not even a willow
Shall swing in the air 'twixt us and our God.
Naked and lone we cross the wide ferry,
Bare to the cold, the dark and the rain.
For here the trail ends.

Here the trail ends.   Here by the landing
I wait the last boat, the slow silent one.
We each go alone — no man with another,
Each into the gloom of the swift black flood —
Boys, it is hard, but here we must scatter;
The gray boatman waits, and I — I go first.
All is dark over there where the dim boat is rocking —
But that is no matter!   No man need to fear;
For clearly we're told the powers that lead us
Shall govern the game to the end of the day.
Good-by — here the trail ends!